INTENTIONAL ACTS

MELISSA F. MILLER

This book is a work of fiction. Names, characters, places, and incidents either are the product of the author's imagination or are used fictitiously.
Any resemblance to actual persons, living or dead, is entirely coincidental.

Published by Brown Street Books.

For more information about the author, please visit www.melissafmiller.com.

ISBN: 978-1-940759-38-8

ALSO BY MELISSA F. MILLER

Want to know when I release a new book?

Go to www.melissafmiller.com to sign up for my email newsletter.

Prefer text alerts? Text BOOKS to 636-303-1088 to receive new release alerts and updates.

The Sasha McCandless Legal Thriller Series

Irreparable Harm

Inadvertent Disclosure

Irretrievably Broken

Indispensable Party

Lovers and Madmen (Novella)

Improper Influence

A Marriage of True Minds (Novella)

Irrevocable Trust

Irrefutable Evidence

A Mingled Yarn (Novella)

Informed Consent

International Incident

Imminent Peril

The Humble Salve (Novella)

The Aroostine Higgins Novels

Critical Vulnerability

Chilling Effect

Calculated Risk

Called Home

The Bodhi King Novels

Dark Path

Lonely Path

Hidden Path

The We Sisters Three Romantic Comedic Mysteries

Rosemary's Gravy

Sage of Innocence

Thyme to Live

Lost and Gowned

1

Meeting of the National Joint Terrorism Task Force
National Counterterrorism Center
McLean, Virginia
Late February

Timothy O'Donnell trailed the Director into the crowded conference room, still wearing his overcoat and warming his cupped hands with his breath.

"It's colder than a witch's t … toothbrush out there," he boomed, catching sight of Ingrid at the last moment, just in time to sanitize his weather commentary.

A handful of the assembled agency and department heads smothered their laughs with fake coughs as they cut their eyes toward Ingrid. But the Director gave no appearance of having noticed any of it. He had his head bent close to his aide and was delivering rapid-fire instructions.

Even given the Director's obliviousness, Ingrid Velder had sufficient experience being the only woman in an endless series of conference rooms to know she needed to get out in front of O'Donnell's comment.

"I believe the saying is colder than a witch's tit, O'Donnell." Her voice carried across the room. She waited a moment for the fresh round of muffled laughter to die down before adding, "And it's not that cold. Back home, it's minus twelve. Now that's cold. Cold enough to freeze the balls off a brass monkey."

O'Donnell roared, pockets of laughter broke out among the country's best and brightest, and even the Director managed a polite chuckle. Despite her doctorate in psychology, Ingrid figured she'd go to her grave not knowing why men found their genitalia so amusing. But, she'd learned long ago that working in a reference to it early in a meeting, briefing, or conference almost always broke the tension.

"It's oddly appropriate that you're all talking about the weather, but let's get started, shall we?" the Director announced with a smile.

He gestured toward the long, polished table, and people hurried to claim seats. Ingrid wrestled a standard-issue black, vinyl chair out from under the table. The chairs were crammed so tightly around the table that the arms touched.

Ingrid had never been one for pomp and circumstance, but she had to admit she was just the tiniest bit disappointed. When she'd seen the agenda and attendee list for this meeting, she'd thought there was an outside chance they'd meet in the secure videoconference room—the one with all the monitors and the shiny, futuristic conference table shaped like an ellipse with one open end. The one where the President received briefings. She'd only ever glimpsed it, but it looked like it belonged on the Starship Enterprise. Instead, this lineup of heavy hitters had been shoehorned into a bland conference room that would fit right in at any mid-priced hotel chain.

She hoped the surroundings weren't a portent of what was to come. She'd been told this meeting was critical and her attendance was necessary. If this turned out to be a discussion about some budgetary hoo-haw or, worse yet, the latest effort to improve morale and retention, she'd have her assistant's head on a pike.

The Director cleared his throat and surveyed the room, interrupting her murderous daydream.

"Thank you all for braving the cold to be here." He paused to smirk at O'Donnell. "A cursory glance around the table ought to confirm the importance of today's meeting. Gentlemen—and Ms. Velder—we're facing a clear and present terroristic threat the likes of which our nation has never seen. The situation is dire. And we need to act quickly. I give you Project Storm Chaser."

On cue, the aide clicked a button on the laptop in front of him and a PowerPoint presentation loaded on the wall-sized screen behind the Director's head.

Project Storm Chaser. Ingrid scribbled the words in her cherry red journal.

She'd used one of the leather-bound day keepers favored by executives the world over until she stumbled on a blog devoted to the bullet journal craze. Now, she kept her appointments, to-do lists, errands, and trackers for how much water she drank and how many criminals she swept off the streets all in one colorful, grid-dotted pocketed journal decorated with whimsical patterned tape and stickers. The incongruity amused her. And as the director of a standing shadow task force, funded by the Department of Homeland Security and tasked with performing those missions too dangerous, too illicit, and too ugly for DHS to acknowledge officially, humor was in short supply in Ingrid's day-to-day existence.

"Storm Chaser? Sounds more like a project for the weather service."

The Director turned toward the speaker, and Ingrid

did, too. Harry Cole, who, like Ingrid, headed a program that officially didn't exist. All she knew was Cole worked with the National Security Agency/Central Security Service and members of the various armed forces' intelligence agencies doing ... something of questionable legality but paramount importance.

"Fair enough, Harry. Seems climate change really *is* dangerous."

The Director waited for the laugh.

The group managed a few weak chuckles.

He went on. "As you surely remember, last year brought us more than our fair share of extreme weather events."

His aide clicked to a list of the catastrophic storms that had hammered the United States, one after another, to the tune of hundreds of billions of dollars' worth of damage. Hurricanes Harvey, Irma, and Maria. A trio of destruction.

"So, what're you saying—ISIL controls the weather now?" Blaine Wilson, the Deputy Director of the CIA's counterterrorism center, wanted to know.

Ingrid reminded herself Wilson was actually FBI, assigned to the CIA as part of the two agencies' work together through the FBI's counterterrorism division. In fact, every person squeezed around the table had a rock-solid pedigree in counterterrorism. Her heart ticked up a beat. This meeting wasn't about the weather.

"No, but it benefits from it. ISIL, Hezbollah, al Qaeda—they all do. Not to mention our homegrown knuckleheads."

O'Donnell drew his eyebrows together. "Benefit how?"

The aide pulled up the next slide, and the Director's neutral expression folded in on itself. He continued with a grimace, "Some of you've been around long enough to remember the aftermath of Katrina back in '05. You may recall we lost track of some folks on the terrorist watch list in the wake of the storm. They got swept up in the evacuations and ended up who-knows-where."

Several heads bobbed, Ingrid's among them.

She'd been working for the FBI's Financial Crimes Section back then. Her investigations had been impacted by the hurricane—shoot, everyone's had. And the Bureau had been in a low-level panic because dozens of targets they'd been tracking were in the wind. 9/11 was still fresh in the populace's memory. There was no way the government could let the media catch wind of the fact that potential terrorists were roaming around the country unaccounted for. There'd been an all hands on deck scramble by the Bureau's National Security Analysis Center (NSAC) to feed flags into the

Investigative Data Warehouse, or IDW, in an effort to find them.

"If memory serves, NSAC eventually caught up with most of them," Wilson volunteered. "The Pentagon was able step up and assist."

"Correct, Blaine. And today, they can't do so, because the Counter-Intelligence Field Agency is no more."

Technically—officially—the Director was right. But every person squeezed around the table knew full well the Pentagon's spies still gathered intelligence on American citizens. And they all also knew the IDW was quaint—a relic compared to the vast network of military, government, and commercial databases the NSAC could now access. But nobody spoke up.

The Director pointed to his final slide. "We're in way worse shape than we were post-Katrina, folks. My people have combed through the databases. Preliminary estimates are that more than six hundred suspects have fallen off our radar since the three storms. Let me repeat, that's six hundred-plus potential terrorists. And we have no idea where they are."

The already-heavy atmosphere of the room grew downright oppressive.

"So Project Storm Chaser—" Ingrid began.

"Is how we're going to find the bastards. Beginning immediately, Project Storm Chaser is the top priority for each of you. We're going to track down every one of these targets. Every last one," the Director finished.

Ingrid closed her journal. Some sixth sense told her she wouldn't want to have a written record of the rest of this meeting.

2

Six weeks later
The Law Offices of McCandless, Volmer & Andrews
Pittsburgh, PA

Sasha McCandless-Connelly gave her legal partner and best friend a blank look.

"Seriously, Mac? You really don't remember? It was my pro bono project last year." Naya tossed her head and made a clicking noise with her tongue.

"Did you just *tsk-tsk* me because I don't remember a client you donated legal services to? Do you know who I represented pro bono last year?"

"There was that guy from Angola seeking asylum—I gave you a hand with his petition. Then you represented the woman who stole her abusive husband's car to escape her marriage. And I think you also did something for the library." She reeled them off.

"Oh."

"Want me to tell you who Will did pro bono work for?"

Sasha took a swig of lukewarm coffee and tried not to shudder at the acidic taste. She desperately needed a warm up—or even better, a fresh mug.

"No need. You've proved your point. I'm sorry I don't remember DoGooderHive or whatever they—"

"DoGiveThrive."

"Right. Sorry." She searched her memory. "Did you help them get their designation as a non-profit charity?"

Naya beamed. "You do remember. Right, I guided them through the application process for their 501(c)(3) tax-exempt status."

Sasha willed her eyes not to glaze over at the reference to the Tax Code. "I sort of remember. In fairness, though, I did have a pretty busy year last year, and I definitely didn't lend *you* a hand. I'd still be having IRS-related nightmares if I had."

"It's all good. Because now they need help with something that's definitely in your wheelhouse."

Naya lifted her chin, and Sasha knew better than to

point out the towering pile of deposition transcripts teetering on the credenza. Or the stack of invoices she needed to review and send out. Or the unearned continuing legal education credits hanging over her head. Or the fact that the twins had pediatrician appointments. She'd baked community service and pro bono work into her firm from the very beginning. She couldn't very well whine that it wasn't convenient this week. Instead, she grabbed her pen and leaned forward.

"Hit me."

"DoGiveThrive received an information request from the feds." She handed Sasha a sheet of paper she'd been waving around.

"A request, not a subpoena?"

"Right."

Sasha scanned the short memo Naya had prepared. Some governmental contractor had wanted the charity to voluntarily search its database against a list of names the government would provide and turn over the results.

"And your—our—client politely told them to go pound salt, right? Please tell me I'm right."

"You're right. They're do-gooders, not idiots."

"So, what's the problem? The government pushed back?"

"Not exactly." She raked her fingers through her hair.

"But about forty-eight hours after they told the feds to kiss their rears, they fell victim to a data breach."

"Ah, that stinks."

"It stinks? It's a freaking disaster!"

"Simmer down. It's probably nowhere near as bad as it looks—at least from a legal perspective. So long as they safeguarded the information using reasonable precautions, they really only need to address the public relations issue. Typically, there's no legal liability unless the company acted intentionally to release private data."

Sasha smiled, happy to have been able to quell Naya's worry so simply. The only problem was, Naya didn't seem remotely reassured. She cut her eyes toward Sasha and pressed her lips together.

"What?" Sasha demanded.

"Would the actions of a rogue employee be considered intentional?"

"A rogue employee? You're telling me DoGiveThrive wasn't the victim of hackers? It was an inside job?"

"Bingo. A programmer who worked for them quit. Apparently on his way out the door, he uploaded all their user data to some paste site, whatever that is."

Sasha's stomach sank to somewhere in the vicinity of her knees and she pressed her fingertips against her temples. "I'll need to do some research. What, if anything, does the data breach have to do with the information request?"

"It's just suspicious—the timing, the programmer's behavior before he quit, I'm not sure what else. They'd like to meet you at their office to explain it all in more detail."

"Before I make any client visits, what exactly is it they want me to do?"

"They need to notify their users about the data breach. They'd like some help with the notification. Obviously, the goal is to avoid being sued. You've got experience guiding clients through recalls. This is similar. And if litigation is threatened, they're going to need help." She held up a hand. "Before you even say it, they know we can't defend a big privacy breach case pro bono. They'll be able to pay a reduced fee. But let's hope it doesn't get to that."

"Since when are you an optimist?"

"Since I promised these guys you'd help them without clearing it with you first." Naya produced her most winning smile.

Sasha laughed despite herself. "Remind me what the business model is here. What kind of information does DoGiveThrive collect, and what do they do with it?"

"They're a twist on a crowdfunding site. People or organizations in need can post projects seeking funding, and then folks can donate small amounts to help them reach their goals."

"Lots of sites do that."

"Sure, but DoGiveThrive differentiates itself on two counts—one, it very carefully vets the recipients of the funds. Some other sites do vetting, too, but these guys really dig deep. The Chief Caring Officer personally visits every potential recipient, sits down with him or her, and hears his or her story. The company also conducts an extensive financial review of every individual or group before they accept them as a site project."

"What's the second thing?" Sasha reached for her coffee mug then reconsidered. She'd hold off until she could get some fresh stuff from the coffee shop downstairs.

"They also guarantee anonymity—for both the recipients *and* the donors. There's no option for either side to know the other. It's like a closed adoption. It's central to the company's mission. They believe to truly give freely, both the donor and the recipient have to remain anonymous."

"So this data breach ..."

Naya nodded. "It's a major violation. Not just of people's private information, but of the company's core promise. The office is in a total uproar. And they have to get out in front of it—fast. Or they'll risk losing the trust of their community."

Sasha's chest tightened. Naya's client had a serious problem, one with the potential to sink the company if it wasn't handled properly. "I don't think they need a lawyer. It sounds like they need a crisis management firm."

"Yeah, well, those don't work pro bono. I told them you're the next best thing—a lawyer who consistently gets herself into and out of crises." Naya laughed shortly, but Sasha didn't hear any humor in it.

"Geez, I'm flattered."

"Come on. I'll walk you out."

Sasha powered down her laptop, packed up her bag, and wriggled into her coat. "Aren't you coming, too? It's your client."

"I know, and I would. But I promised Will I'd pitch in on the briefs you were supposed to be working on for his foreign bribery case."

She'd entirely forgotten her promise to help Will. She was already overextended—what was one more major case? "Fine, but we're stopping by Jake's and you're buying me a fresh coffee for the road."

"Puh-lease. Do I look like I'm new here? I already called down and put in your order. And since when do you pay for coffee at Jake's?"

"Good point. Lucky for us we know a pro bono coffee shop owner."

This time, Naya's laughter rang true. "Pro bono, my sweet behind. Jake builds the cost of your caffeine addiction right into the lease."

Sasha nodded. It could very well be true. And worth every penny.

3

TOP-SECRET CONFIDENTIAL
FOR YOUR EYES ONLY

DISTRIBUTION LIST: Project Storm Chaser Task Force Members

STATUS UPDATE

Phase One has been completed. The Project Storm Chaser Task Force has run queries for all missing targets' names and known aliases across all one hundred and thirty databases maintained by our governmental, military, state, and commercial partners, including but not limited to all files maintained by NSAC. As teams continue to comb through the hits obtained from this initial search, Phase Two of the project is being implemented on a rolling basis.

Select contractors have been provided subsets of the initial search results and the lists of targets and advised to hone in on their current locations. Contractors were advised to prioritize this project.

All Task Force members should identify teams internal to their departments who will be on call and ready to interview, detail, and, if necessary, neutralize identified targets.

Further details will be disseminated on a need-to-know basis.

Across town, in an undisclosed location, Ingrid read the short memorandum, re-read it, and put it face down on the top of the pile of documents to be shredded at the end of the day. Then she turned her attention back to the pair of men standing in her makeshift office.

"Where are we on the James matter?"

Hank Richardson glanced at his second-in-command before answering. "Ma'am, Leo has compiled a pretty thorough dossier on Mr. James. He seems to be clean—at least as far as the counterfeiting is concerned."

Beside him, Leo Connelly nodded his agreement.

Ingrid couldn't hide her surprise. "Really? His brother hasn't contacted him at all?"

"Not once," Connelly confirmed. "Milton James may need someone to run his criminal enterprise while he's behind bars, but I don't think he's tapped his brother for that role."

"Why on earth not?" Ingrid muttered more to herself than to Richardson and Connelly.

Connelly cleared his throat and answered anyway. "Milton may have found out his younger brother's been ... comforting his wife while he's serving his sentence."

"Paul James is sleeping with his sister-in-law?"

"Affirmative."

Ingrid shook her head. "Well, I suppose once Milton's released, he'll kill them both, and we'll get to put him away again."

Richardson chuckled then shifted his weight. "So, do you want us to close the Paul James matter and see if we can gather any intel on who *is* minding the store for Milton?"

She nodded absently. “Yes.” Her gaze fell on the upside-down memo. “But don’t get too wrapped up in it. You’re both—we’re all—on standby and could receive a priority assignment any day. Straight from NCTC.”

Hank whistled, a long, low note. “Want to give us the background?”

“Can’t. This is a top-secret, need-to-know project.”

The men exchanged a look.

She pursed her lips and weighed how much to divulge. Richardson was her most trusted deputy. He headed her only standing task force. And Connelly was *his* most trusted deputy. They’d run more successful operations out of the Pittsburgh office than the rest of her department combined. But, still, there was a limit to what she was able to share at this point.

She chose her words with care. “Analysts have been running algorithms on *a lot* of information from the databases. Now they’re reaching out to private entities to do the same. Once they’ve had a chance to dig into all the data and analyze and categorize it, I suspect we’re—you’re—going to be busy.”

“Busy how, ma’am? Interviews? Surveillance?” Connelly asked.

They all knew the real question was unasked, buried under the words he’d said.

"Sure. But possibly more complicated work. It could get messy."

It was as much as she could say. But it was plenty.

Richardson raised his eyebrows. A muscle twitched in Connelly's left cheek.

After a moment's silence, Richardson coughed. "And messy work's been authorized?"

"Nothing's been authorized yet. But the scope of this project goes up to and includes neutralizing confirmed threats."

Ingrid locked eyes with each man in turn. None of them spoke. They all intellectually understood their department's mission could require them to take a human life. And she knew both men had, in fact, fired their weapons in the line of duty.

But assassination was different. It wasn't a reaction to a threat encountered in the field. It was a calculated decision to eliminate a potential threat. It was playing God. And she prayed to God neither of them would be called upon to do it. But if one them was, then he would. It was that simple.

She waited another ten seconds for the message to sink in.

"You're dismissed."

4

Sasha watched from DoGiveThrive's floor-to-ceiling window as the urban drama spooled out on the other side of the reclaimed green space (also known as a lawn) below. A harried-looking blonde woman pushing a double stroller and holding the hand of a preschool-aged boy was yelling at an equally harried-looking balding guy in a business suit. The suit guy had managed to jam his BMW into an almost-big enough parking spot, scraping the front bumper of the woman's dirty minivan in the process. She was shaking a finger at the man as if she were scolding one of her kids. He was puffing out his chest as if he were some alpha gorilla in the wild. Sasha turned away from the scene before he could beat his fists on his torso.

Luckily, the company's headquarters was walking

distance from her office. Her route had taken her through Shadyside and the ever-evolving hipster sections of East Liberty. The stroll had given her time to drink her coffee and clear her head. And she hadn't had to engage in mortal combat over a parking spot. Win. Win. And win.

"Ms. McCandless-Connelly? Will you come with me?" The receptionist blinked at her from behind his round eyeglasses.

The two-toned acetate frames made him seem even younger than he was. He smiled, and she half-expected him to be missing a front tooth, he was so boyish-looking. She wasn't surprised. A non-profit, online crowd-funding startup was likely to be staffed by young idealists.

She stood and slung her bag over her shoulder. He ushered her around a glass block wall that seemed to serve no structural purpose.

As he led her down a bright hallway, he apologized. "Gella's sorry she kept you waiting. Things have just been bananas around here."

"I can imagine."

She caught a glimpse of a warren of standing desks through a glass wall. A gaggle of people wearing head-sets raced from station to station, showing each other their tablet displays.

"What's going on in there?"

"Damage control. We have teams of charity sherpas reaching out to members of our tribe."

Charity sherpas? Tribe? She needed a translator, and fast.

"Um ..."

The unflappable receptionist turned and flashed her a smile. "Every project is assigned two charity sherpas—one sherpa works with the recipient, and the other interfaces with the donors. Recipients and donors are all considered members of our global DoGiveThrive tribe."

"Does the donor sherpa know the identity of the recipient, and does the recipient sherpa know who the donors are?"

"Oh, no. That's strictly compartmentalized. The sherpas tend to their own side of the relationship only."

"Hmm." She faked a smile and tried to untangle the possible reasons for the seemingly excessive secrecy.

"Here we are," he chirped and swept his arm toward an open door to usher her inside ahead of him.

A woman in her late fifties sat behind a squat, highly polished desk. She wore a suit that would blend right in at any law firm and a chunky pearl choker. The effect was jarring. Her executive suite furniture and corporate appearance were at odds with her modernistic surroundings and her youthful, casually dressed employees—the majority of whom sported multiple piercings and colorful tattoos.

The woman stood. Her broad smile filled her face and her eyes disappeared into their surrounding laugh lines. She stepped forward to shake Sasha's hand.

"I'm Gella Pinkney. Thank you for coming on such short notice, Ms. McCandless-Connelly."

"Call me Sasha. McCandless-Connelly's a mouthful."

She laughed. "A bit. Would you like something to drink, Sasha?"

"No, thanks."

The receptionist stood waiting with his hands clasped in front of him.

"That'll be all, Devon." She dismissed him with another warm smile.

"Let me know if you ladies need anything," he said as he backed out of the room and pulled the door closed with a soft thud.

"Please, make yourself comfortable." Gella Pinkney gestured toward a pair of high-backed chairs arranged in front of her desk.

Sasha took a seat in the chair on the left and reached into her bag for a legal pad and pen. Gella sat down across from her and crossed her ankles. The only traces of urgency the woman betrayed were her slight lean forward and the shadows under her eyes.

"I'm so grateful to Naya—and you. We desperately need some guidance. I never imagined something like this could happen. And, frankly, I'm at a loss. We want to do the right thing here—we just don't know what it is."

Sasha made a sympathetic sound in her throat then said, "I know you're extremely busy putting out fires, but it would be helpful for me to get clear on the company's background before we turn to the issue of the data breach."

"Okay." Gella exhaled slowly as if she were releasing the air from a balloon. "DoGiveThrive was the result of a vision I had during my last semester of divinity school."

"When was that?"

"Just three years ago. I felt called to serve late in life, after my children were grown and out on their own. I'd taught elementary school before my husband and I started our family, but when I thought about going back to the classroom, it felt like a poor fit. So I entered the seminary."

"And you were about to graduate when you came up with the idea for the nonprofit?"

"Yes. I was sitting in contemplation, thinking about how our digital world has turned neighbors into strangers and, conversely, turned strangers half a world apart into friends."

Sasha nodded to prompt her to continue.

Gella stood and walked over to a tall, wide cabinet that filled the wall opposite her desk. She pulled open the doors, fed them into tracks that pulled them back into the cabinet's interior, and revealed a digital map of the world. She pressed a button and clusters of digital hearts materialized over the land masses.

"At DoGiveThrive we curate projects from around the globe that donors feel drawn to support. And we don't just give our recipients financial support; we work to restore their dignity and preserve their privacy. It's what makes us different. It's what makes us *us*." Gella's practiced speech gave way as her voice broke with emotion.

"Why is privacy so important to you?"

Gella's hand fluttered to her throat. She splayed her fingers against her collarbone. "How did you know?"

"Know what?" Sasha shook her head.

"I'm ... sorry. You caught me by surprise. Privacy is central to our mission because we believe publicly identifying someone as a 'charity case' has a chilling effect for members of certain religious, cultural, and ethnic communities. It stops folks from asking for help they may truly need. *And* we believe generosity is its own reward. Studies have shown purely altruistic giving—giving anonymously, without any hope of enhancing the donor's social standing—activates powerful centers in the brain. But, at the same time, it's been shown having an identifiable beneficiary increases giving, and being able to see the effect of one's gift is gratifying. So, we created the sherpas and the tribes to connect people without revealing their actual identities. It's a balancing act."

For all Gella's polished delivery and self-assuredness, Sasha sensed there was more to the company's focus on anonymity.

"And there's no other reason for your confidentiality pledge?" She kept her voice gentle, but her eyes bored into the older woman.

A long silence stretched out between them.

Sasha waited.

Gella stared unblinkingly at her digital map.

Finally, she sighed. "This is a personal story. It's not something I share."

"Anything you tell me is covered by attorney-client privilege. Unless you're planning to commit a crime. In which case, please don't tell me."

Gella laughed a soft, sad laugh. "No, it's nothing like that. My oldest daughter, she was living out west and got involved with a man. She thought she'd met her soulmate. Then he turned violent. She sought a protection from abuse order and got it. It didn't stop him. She ran, hid at a women's shelter. He found her. When my husband and I found out, we went and got her. We brought her home."

"I'm so sorry."

"Our daughter's fortunate. She's not on social media. And she has us to help her start over. But a woman she'd met at the shelter didn't have the same resources we did. Her family posted a fundraising request on one of the other sites to raise the money to get her out of the relationship. And ...." She broke off and looked down at her hands, as if surprised to see herself wringing them, over and over, as though she were washing them.

"And he found her through the site?"

Gella nodded wordlessly.

"So, you want to protect the recipients."

"And the donors. My daughter, for instance. If she wants to give to a cause, she has to worry. Will her name be published? There are a lot of people who have privacy concerns. It's not just victims of domestic violence."

"I understand."

She *did* understand. Because of their work, she and Connelly kept their personal details locked down. And yet Connelly's estranged father had found them through a publicly accessible PDF of a church bulletin.

Gella cleared her throat. "A secondary concern is the venom some people freely spew online. If you look at the other crowdfunding sites, you'll see horrible comments posted by complete strangers. Death threats, mockery, terrible insults directed about both those raising the funds and those donating. And even if the platform doesn't enable comments, committed trolls search the internet, find people's social media profiles and drag them through the mud there. It's poisonous. Our procedures protect our tribe members. They aren't subject to hate because they have a need ... or a heart. They count on that. It's part of our pledge to them. And now ... we've broken that pledge."

"Because of the data breach?"

"Yes."

Sasha studied the CEO. Tears had filled her eyes while she'd told the story about her daughter's friend, but now her blue eyes were steely and determined.

"We'll make it right, Gella. Tell me how it happened."

"Right. So last week, we received the request from the NCTC—"

"Hang on. What's the NCTC?"

"The National Counterterrorism Center? Something

like that. They're located outside D.C., in Northern Virginia."

Sasha scrawled on her notepad: *Ask LC re: NCTC.* After all, what good was having a G-man for a husband if a girl couldn't pick his brain from time to time?

"Okay. And the request came from this NCTC directly?"

Gella wrinkled her forehead. "No. Actually it came from a contractor." She walked to her desk and flipped through a tidy stack of papers. "It was an outfit called Sentinel Solution Systems. Also with a Virginia address."

Sasha noted the name. "Go on."

"We obviously declined to provide the information they requested."

"And what exactly did they ask for? Naya mentioned a list of names."

"Yeah, they sent us a list of, oh, about fifty names. They wanted us to query our database and see if there were any matches between their list and our donors or our recipients. Obviously, we refused."

"Fifty names. And they specifically asked you to query both subsets?" Sasha mused.

"Well, no. I'm not sure they know how, or even that, we segregate our data. They asked for 'all customer files.' I'm sure it was a boilerplate request. I mean, we don't consider any members of our tribe to be 'customers.'"

"Sure. I'll need copies of all the correspondence."

"Of course." She pressed a button on her phone.

"Yes?" A breathy voice came through the speaker instantly.

"Elizabelle, Ms. McCandless-Connelly is going to need a copy of everything in the data breach file."

"Got it," Elizabelle promised.

"Thanks." Gella released the intercom button. "There's not much in the file. And, to be completely honest, I'm not sure how helpful you'll find any of it."

"It's all helpful. Trust me." Even after fifteen years of legal practice, Sasha remained amazed at how the outcome of a case could turn on the most seemingly trivial piece of information.

"I'll take your word for it." Gella returned to her chair across from Sasha. "In any case, we sent our response to Sentinel Solution Systems via email on Friday afternoon, and we put a hard copy in the mail. Monday morning, at eight o'clock sharp, Asher Morgan, our senior programmer, called in and quit over the phone."

"He didn't even come in and clean out his ... wherever your people keep their personal stuff?" It occurred to Sasha that the rows of standing desks Devon had led her past had all lacked drawers.

"We don't keep personal effects in our communal spaces, but every team member has a lock box. And apparently, Asher cleared out his lock box over the weekend. The keyless entry system recorded him logging in Sunday evening, shortly after six p.m. He left just before ten o'clock. No one else was in the space during that stretch of time."

"And the data went up on the ... um ... paste site over the weekend?"

"To the best of our knowledge, yes. Elizabelle was our junior programmer—now she's our only programmer. She's the one who found the breach. She'll be able to explain the technical stuff better than I can."

Gella stood again and headed for the door. Sasha tossed her legal pad back into her bag and trailed behind her.

ELIZABELLE DIDN'T WORK in the pen with the charity sherpas. She had a private office not much smaller than Gella's, although it was more Swedish modular furniture, less dark wood. It also had been, until quite recently, a semi-private office.

A second work station was set up in the far corner of the room. Here, too, Sasha noted there were no desk drawers. Just wide work spaces filled with computer equipment. Elizabelle looked up from one of the oversized monitors when Gella and Sasha came around the Asian screen that functioned as an ad hoc door.

"Hi, there." She popped a thumb drive out of a USB port and stood up. "I'm Elizabelle. You must be Ms. McCandless-Connelly. Here are your files. They're all PDFs." She pressed the drive into Sasha's palm in lieu of shaking hands.

"Thanks. Elizabelle's a pretty name."

The programmer twisted her long red hair into a knot on the top of her head then adjusted her thick, black-framed glasses. "Yeah. My parents couldn't agree. One mom wanted Isabelle. My other mom wanted Elizabeth. After a four-day standoff, during which they either called me 'it' or 'the baby,' they compromised."

Sasha laughed, disarmed by the woman's frank friendliness.

Gella beamed at Elizabelle. "Elizabelle's a gem. She was the fifth programmer we hired to help Asher. And the only one to survive more than a month."

"Wow. How long did you work with him?"

"Five hundred and thirty-seven days. But who's

counting?" She quirked her mouth into the barest hint of a smile.

"That bad, huh?"

Gella coughed. "Asher was very talented. But, unfortunately, he knew it. To say he was prickly would be an insult to porcupines."

"Not to mention cacti," Elizabelle cracked.

"He sounds like a real sweetheart. Has anyone called for a reference?"

"Nope. And I don't expect anyone will. Elizabelle is connected with him on some IT professional network. He updated his profile on Monday afternoon to list Sentinel Solution Systems as his employer."

"Then he promptly un-peered me and blocked me." Elizabelle snorted.

"Wait. He went to work for the contractor who requested the data?"

"Evidently."

"That's nervy."

"That's Asher," Gella explained.

Sasha scrunched up her forehead. "I'm confused. If he was going to join the company, why leak the data publicly? Why not just put it on a drive and take it with him?"

Elizabelle was nodding. "You'd have to know Asher for it to make sense. He was so chapped when Gella announced that the company wouldn't be complying with the information request. Like, pretty much everything irritated him, but that news had him *incensed.*"

"He thought DoGiveThrive should've just handed over user data that it promised it would keep private?"

The programmer blew out a long breath. "Yeah. So, Asher was an odd duck. He called himself a libertarian, but he was pretty hardcore about national security. He took one look at the list of names from Sentinel Solution Systems and announced that they were trying to track down terrorists."

"Based on the names?" Sasha asked careful to keep her tone neutral.

"Right."

"Is there a list of the requested names on this drive?"

"Yep."

"Good. Oh, wait. I have another question. Even though the company decided not to comply with the request, did you and Asher run the names anyway? Just to satisfy your curiosity?"

Elizabelle pressed her lips into a thin line and shifted her gaze to a point over Sasha's shoulder.

So, that's a yes. But she needed to hear it from the client.

"Listen, anything you tell me is confidential. It really doesn't matter how bad the facts are, as long as you disclose them. The only way anything you say could hurt the company is if you aren't completely honest. I need to know."

Elizabelle chewed on a ragged cuticle.

"She's right. Whatever it is, just tell us," Gella urged. "And don't bite your nails."

"Okay, look. I didn't run the names. And I didn't know that Asher did, but he must've done it on Friday. I came back from my lunchtime yoga class and he jumped about a mile when I walked into the room. He started screaming at me about sneaking up on him. He tossed his takeout coffee on the floor and said I'd startled him. But … I think he made the mess just to distract me. Because while I was running around looking for a mop, he turned off his display."

"Can't you look at his, I don't know, keystroke log or something and know for sure?" Sasha asked.

"If it was one of the sherpas or one of you two, sure. But Asher knew what he was doing. He wiped everything from the system—I mean, every trace of his activity in the past week is gone. Poof. Like it never happened."

That would make establishing his liability hard. Maybe impossible. Sasha swore under her breath.

"Why don't you tell Sasha about the paste?" Gella said.

Elizabelle leaned across her desk and tapped her mouse to wake up her computer. "So, after Gella told me Asher quit I started to poke around. Well, first I did a happy dance. *Then* I started poking around in his files. That's when I learned that he'd covered his tracks. The only reason he'd do that was if he had something to hide. I mean, he was a jerk but he wasn't a petty jerk. He wasn't the type to change everybody's passwords on the way out the door or anything. And to answer your question about why he didn't just put the stuff on a drive and take it with him, I think he wanted to do it publicly, through a pastebin, for what do you lawyers call it—plausible deniability?"

Sasha nodded glumly. "So now, if Sentinel Solution Systems just *happens* to come into possession of the leaked data they can say they happened upon it on the Internet."

"Bingo."

"So this site, it's a hacker thing?"

"Not really. Pastebin or text storage sites are super common. They're hosting sites that people like me use to review code with other programmers. You copy the source code and paste it into the site as straight text. Then peers can either inspect the code or troubleshoot it or whatever through an IRC—sorry, that's an Internet Relay Chat. The whole process is kind of antiquated, to tell you the truth. I mean, it's older than *I* am."

Sasha was pretty sure she had shoes that were older than Elizabelle. Elizabelle's fingers flew over the keyboard, and she pulled up a website. She squinted at the white background. It had a distinctly 1990s feel. Clunky, plain, and uninspired. No theme, no video, not even a header picture. Sasha half expected to hear the 'you've got mail' *ding* she remembered from her middle school years when her parents would check their email on the family PC.

"So this is it—the text storage site?"

"Yes." She clicked a hyperlink on the right side of the page and a snippet of gibberish appeared in a box in the center of the page.

"So, it's for coders? Not hackers?"

"Well, the sites originated as places to share code. But anonymous posters—leakers, whistleblowers, anyone who has a reason to hide their identity—have been using pastebin sites for years to post information. Sometimes that information includes sensitive data, and, yes, sometimes it's been obtained by methods that you would probably call 'hacking.' But you have to understand the ethos in the programmer community. Hacking doesn't have a strictly negative connotation. There's white hat hacking to reveal vulnerabilities so they can be fixed. There's disseminating information to counter government propaganda. And there's black hat hacking, too, of course."

Elizabelle paused and looked over her shoulder as if to confirm Sasha and Gella were following her train of thought. They both nodded.

She continued, "There are also all sorts of random postings. Posts range from recipes to creative writing to detailed rants about conspiracy theories. You could stumble across just about anything, really."

She clicked through several hyperlinks and the text in the central box changed from a snippet of code to a poem to a string of digits to what appeared to be a manifesto. All the entries were titled 'Untitled.'

"And you found the data Asher leaked here on this site?" Gella asked.

"Yeah. Once I realized he'd messed with our local servers and the remote backups, I got curious. So, I clicked through a hot mess of links from Sunday night until I found this." She closed out of the browser and opened an image on her desktop.

Gella inhaled sharply.

"Don't worry. I took a screenshot and then immediately messaged the developer who runs the site and had it taken down within minutes."

"Good work. And quick thinking." The programmer's fast response would go a long way toward minimizing DoGiveThrive's exposure.

She ducked her head and shrugged off Sasha's praise. "Thanks. I know the guy—I met him at a conference last year. But, he did say it was up for about ten hours."

Gella turned to Sasha with worried eyes. "That's bad, right?"

"It's going to depend on how many views it had. And how many downloads or copies were made. And by whom. Will your friend be able to tell us that, Elizabelle?"

"Will he be able to? Sure. Will he? I can't say for sure. This crowd embraces the idea that information wants to be freely available. Like, taking down the data was one thing. Ratting out everyone who looked at it ... that may be further than he's willing to go, you know?"

Sasha did know. But it was not the answer she'd hoped for. "Okay. Gella and I will craft a legal strategy to get that information from the hosting site through the courts, if necessary. But in the meantime, could you approach him as a friend? Explain *why* this breach is so bad from the company's perspective, try to persuade him?"

Elizabelle flashed a bright smile. "I'll give it a shot."

"Good. Don't put anything in writing to him. But

after you talk, jot down some notes to memorialize your conversation."

She nodded her understanding.

"Do you need anything else from Elizabelle? She's pretty busy right now," Gella pointed out.

"Just one more question. I'm looking at this screenshot and it appears your users' names and zip codes were revealed. Is that all Asher leaked?"

"Is that *all?*" Gella was aghast.

Sasha raised both hands to slow her down before she got whipped up. "I know your business model promises anonymity. But from a crisis management perspective, things could be much, much worse. He could have posted full addresses, telephone numbers, passwords. Or social security numbers, credit card numbers. I mean, he didn't even match the names to the projects they funded or benefited from, did he?"

She understood why DoGiveThrive was spiraling into a panic, but the truth was this breach really didn't lend itself to real liability. Actual, provable damages stemming from the leak seemed out of the question.

Gella exhaled. "Yes, I suppose that's all true. But this still feels like a terrible violation."

"It is. And we're going to harness that emotion you're feeling when we communicate the breach to your tribe. But, for instance, I would normally suggest you offer free credit monitoring for the affected users. In this case, there's no way a name and a zip code is going to expose anyone to credit fraud or identity fraud. Trust me, this is not as awful as it seems."

Both women instantly brightened. Gella rolled her neck. The tension in the room dissipated. Sasha gave herself a moment to revel in the rare feeling of delivering good news to a client without a corresponding giant legal bill.

What she couldn't have known, though, was she was wrong. Dead wrong.

5

Leo realized he'd been staring blankly at the painting hanging on the dining room wall above Sasha's head. He blinked and gave his head a little shake.

"Sorry, were you saying something?"

She narrowed her eyes and studied his face. "What's wrong with you?"

He sucked in a breath. He had to pull himself together. His wife was many things, but chief among them, was perceptive as *hell.* She was impossible to surprise, impossible to evade, and, to top it off, she was tenacious. If she suspected something was troubling him and, worse, that he was hiding it from her, she'd be after him like she was Mocha and he was a hambone.

He spared a glance at their lazy retriever snoozing in

the kitchen with the cat curled around his tail. Scratch that. Mocha was too well-fed and pampered to pursue food the way Sasha would pursue information.

"Earth to Connelly."

He shook his head again. She'd use her lawyer lie-detecting superpowers to tell if he made something up. Better to go with a kernel of the truth and then dance away from the topic.

"Sorry. I'm just a little distracted. Hank and I met with the boss today."

She paused, her wine glass halfway to her lips. "Ingrid Velder's in town? I thought she only visited you and Hank once a month."

"Usually, she does."

Worry sparked in her green eyes. "What's going on? Why is she here?"

He took a drink before answering. "She didn't stay. She was in town two hours, tops. It's crazy that the department pays to maintain an office for her here, when you think about it."

"Connelly ..." Her voice held a warning.

"What?"

"We have a rare adults-only dinner. No twins. No forks to pick up off the floor. No need to scrape potatoes off the table when we're done. We're eating in the *dining room*, for crying out loud. Do you think I want to squander this brief miracle on a conversation about the government's wasteful use of our tax dollars? Spoiler: no, I do not. The whole reason I even let Maisy take Finn and Fiona to the arts and movement festival was so we could reconnect. You know, have an actual conversation. Remember those?"

He chuckled. "It's hazy, but I think I have a distant memory. I seem to recall finding it enjoyable."

Her bow lips curved into a smile. "Good. So, let's talk. Lord knows Maisy's going to bring them home sticky, stuffed with treats, and overstimulated."

"From an arts and movement festival for preschoolers?"

"It's Maisy," she countered.

He laughed again. It felt almost genuine this time. "Point taken."

"So? What did Ingrid want?"

The laughter died in his throat. He tensed his shoulders. There was zero chance he was going to spend their romantic, kid-free dinner explaining that he'd been put on notice that he might be asked to kill someone, no questions asked, in the near future.

Make that a less than zero chance he was going to talk to her about that prospect—and not only because doing so would be divulging sensitive national security information. No, the conversation would devolve into a massive fight if he so much as hinted at the choices the government was sometimes forced to make in order to protect the country.

He waved his hand in the air. "Oh, just bureaucratic stuff. She needed to go over some budget stuff with Hank. And you know Hank, he wasn't going to suffer alone. So he roped me into the meeting."

He forked a chunk of potatoes into his mouth and chewed slowly, watching her watch him over the rim of her wineglass.

"Hmm."

He swallowed and lifted the decanter of merlot. "More wine?"

She nodded and pushed her glass toward him. He refilled hers then topped off his own glass.

"Thanks. If I didn't know better, I'd think you were trying to make me tipsy ... or change the subject."

"Good thing you know better." He raised his glass.

"Mmm-hmm."

"Did *you* have any interesting meetings today?"

"Nothing that could compete with a budgetary review, I'm sure. But I actually did meet with a new client. Well, new to me. It's one of Naya's transactional clients."

He felt the tension in his neck and back ease a half a notch at the welcome distraction. He'd been replaying Ingrid's parting words in a loop for what felt like hours. If Sasha could displace them with a story about some corporate issue, he might even get some sleep tonight.

"Are they suing someone? Or being sued?"

"Neither, yet. Possibly both, eventually. They're a pro bono client; Naya helped them get their charitable tax-exempt status from the IRS last year. They do anonymous crowdfunding for vetted charity projects."

"Sounds cool."

"It's a pretty decent model. I mean, it's wildly hipster. They have offices in East Liberty in one of those loft-type spaces. All glass block and open work corrals. No doors, no desk drawers."

"Average age, twelve and a half?"

"Exactly. Well, except for the CEO. Gella's probably only about five or six years younger than my mom. After her kids were grown, she enrolled in divinity school, which is where she had her vision about this charitable giving model."

Leo finished his last bite of roasted carrots. "The hipster work environment aside, it doesn't sound like an outfit that could've pissed off someone badly enough to need your services."

She pushed her plate away as she warmed to her topic. "So they promise their users—sorry, their tribe—

complete anonymity. On both sides of the transactions. It's part of their core mission."

"Why?"

"Long story, but mainly to protect people's privacy from Internet trolls and, you know, any enemies they may have in real life."

"Enemies?"

"Stalkers, vengeful exes. Nothing too crazy."

He stuck out his lower lip and nodded his head. It wasn't the worst idea to limit one's virtual footprint if it could be done.

"So if they don't make their users public and presumably don't sell their data to advertisers, how do they pay the light bill?"

"A portion of each donation does go to operating expenses, but they run lean. Their numbers are good."

He made a mental note to talk to the Kurcks about their next project. Naya's client might be a good partner for the big anti-human trafficking initiative he, Elli, and Oliver were planning.

"Got it. So what happened?"

"A disgruntled employee uploaded a list of their users to a text storage site where it was publicly available for at least ten hours."

He groaned. "Let me guess, credit card numbers, home addresses, dates of birth, the whole ball of wax?"

He was surprised when she laughed. "Nope. Full names and zip codes. That's it."

"Seriously?"

"Apparently, the data is compartmentalized internally so the charity sherpas—"

"Come again?"

"Two internal employees are assigned to each project. They call them sherpas. Anyway, one employee works with the donor. The other works with the recipient. They only know the identities of the people on their side of the transaction. The donations and the disbursements are processed through a third-party processor, so identifying financial information isn't retained on their local systems. At the end of the year, the payment processor sends a file with the information the company needs to issue tax documents. Those are stored in hard copy in a safe in Gella's office."

"So, this hack or leak was really no big deal? I mean, presumably the leaker was fired, but beyond that, no harm, no foul. Right?"

"That's how it looks. The programmer who uploaded the list quit, so he can't be fired. What he did was obviously wrong, but unless the company incurs some actual damage, they probably don't even have grounds to sue him."

"So the biggest issue is reputational. The breach

could damage their fundraising efforts, right? If they make a point of the fact that they facilitate truly anonymous giving, and that's been called into question by this jagoff, couldn't they sue?"

She beamed at him. "Mr. Connelly, you may've missed your calling. That's a solid legal analysis."

"No thanks. I'll take chasing bad guys over reading deposition transcripts any day." He snorted.

"Your loss. Anyway, yes, if they get a black eye in the charitable crowdfunding community, they can go after this guy and his new employer. But I helped Gella craft a pretty strong apology message to their users. And the charity sherpas are personally calling every single person to explain what happened using a script I gave them. If they manage this right, honestly, it just demonstrates that they're human beings. But also, it's a chance for them to show that they take privacy seriously and are committed to fixing the vulnerabilities in their system that allowed this to happen in the first place. I feel like it could be a public relations win in the end. Or at least, a neutral event."

She reached across the table and began stacking the dirty plates. She was halfway to the kitchen with them when the hole in her story hit him.

"Wait. Why'd he do it? What was the point of leaking a bunch of names and zips? Just to be a dick?"

He screwed up his forehead. It didn't make a lick of sense.

She pivoted, resting the dishes against her hip, and looked back at him. "Actually, we have a theory about his motivation, but it's farfetched. Let me load the dishwasher and then I'll pick your brain while we finish off the wine. Deal?"

"You're on."

He swept up the wineglasses and the decanter and moved to the pair of chairs in front of the fireplace. While she banged around in the kitchen, he congratulated himself for successfully evading any further questions about Ingrid. Then he resolved to push the subject of Ingrid firmly out of his mind for the remainder of the evening.

Sasha returned from the kitchen bearing a fancy silver tray they'd received as a wedding gift. "Look honey, I made dessert."

"You broke a dark chocolate bar into pieces."

"It's my specialty."

He plucked a square of chocolate from the proffered tray and popped it into his mouth. Then he handed her wine to her as she sank into the chair across from him.

"My brain's all yours. Pick away."

"Eww." She wrinkled her nose. After a sip of merlot, curled her legs up under her and leaned toward him.

"Okay, the rogue programmer went to work for a company called Sentinel Solution Systems. It's in Arlington, Virginia. Ever hear of it?"

He searched his memory. "No. Should I have?"

"I'm not sure. They're a government contractor."

He laughed so hard he choked on his chocolate. She pounded him on the back.

"Sorry," he said when he could breathe. "Do you have any idea how many hundreds, no thousands, of government contractors there are? I don't know every one."

She rolled her eyes. "I thought you might have run into these guys, though. They do work for the National Counterterrorism Center, whatever that is. Based solely on the name, they sound like a group you might have run into a time or two."

Leo took a long drink of wine to rinse the chocolate out of his mouth. He took his time about it, too, so he could frame his response. He had to be forthcoming enough to satisfy her lawyer sensibilities but vague enough that she'd lose interest in the line of inquiry.

"Sure, I know the NCTC. But they use loads of contractors. Desk jockeys who analyze computer files all day, searching for needles in digital haystacks. It's probably even more boring than being a litigator."

She appraised him for several long seconds. He looked back at her, blank faced.

Finally, she nodded. She nibbled on a square of chocolate then said, "This leaker going to work for this particular NCTC contractor was a weird coincidence, though."

"Why's that?" His voice was lazy. The wine was starting to make him tired.

"Last week, Sentinel sent a letter to my client asking them to voluntarily provide information to assist in some investigation."

The words chilled him as thoroughly as a pitcher of ice water being poured over his head. "They did? Did your client comply?" he asked, suddenly alert.

"Are you *kidding*? Of course not."

"You do realize the NCTC works round the clock to prevent another major terror attack on U.S. soil, right? And that without cooperation from the civil sector, their job becomes much harder—some might even say impossible?"

She gave him a flat look. "Connelly, let's not rehash this argument, okay? Just like you're not going to wake up one morning convinced that the Constitutionally protected right to privacy is more important than defending the homeland, I'm not ever going to think it's smart for anyone—whether they're an individual or a corporation—to hand over private information to the government just because they asked nicely. Benjamin Franklin put it best, 'They that can give up essential liberty to obtain a little safety deserve neither liberty nor safety.'"

He hated what he was about to say. He knew it would annoy her. He told himself not to do it.

And, yet, the words left his mouth, seemingly of their own accord. "Yes, that's what's inscribed on the Statue of Liberty, and, yes, it's attributed to Franklin. But it's a misinterpretation of what old Ben actually said. In a 1755 letter, he wrote 'Those who would give up essential Liberty, to purchase a little temporary Safety, deserve neither Liberty nor Safety.' The letter was written in the middle of a power struggle over whether the Pennsylvania assembly had the power to tax William Penn's land. So, it's not really on point."

She stared at him.

"American History major, you know, I couldn't help myself."

She closed her eyes for a nanosecond then said, "I can't do this with you right now, Connelly. Your super interesting factoid notwithstanding, that quote has a long history of being used to defend our right to liberty. It's not engraved on the symbol of America because of some tax dispute that predates the formation of the country. You know that, right?"

He did. He also knew that when she flushed from her chest all the way up to her cheeks, he was dangerously close to sleeping on the couch. He watched the red stain travel from her collar line up her neck and contemplated whether it was too late for damage control.

"I'm sorry, I shouldn't have interrupted you. Why don't you go on?"

She gave him a long, cool look. "Fine. So, no, my client didn't voluntarily provide the information the NCTC wanted, which apparently upset the programmer. They think he leaked the list of names so this Sentinel outfit would find it."

"That's a pretty big assumption."

She shrugged, conceding the point. "Can you think of any reason the NCTC would want a charitable organization to confirm whether any people on a list of names had donated to or received a donation from one of its campaigns?"

He could think of dozens. None of them were reasons he planned to share with his fiery bride. "I suppose it depends on the names."

She sighed. "I guess you're right."

He rested his glass on the tray and reached for her hand. As he rubbed his thumb over hers, he said, "I know you don't like advice, especially the unsolicited kind. But because I love you, and I'd selfishly like you to stay alive and unincarcerated, I'm going to give you some anyway. Do not mess with the NCTC."

She rolled her eyes.

"I mean it. Promise me you won't get anyone there riled up."

"As the parent of toddlers, you know as well as I do, that I can't control anyone else's emotional reactions. All I can do is control my own actions."

He managed a half-smirk as she parroted the latest piece of wisdom she'd picked up from one of her parenting books.

"Does that mean you're promising to behave?"

She leaned over and kissed him lightly. He pulled her onto his lap and kissed her back, not at all lightly, the question already forgotten.

Sasha sat on the edge of her bed and watched Connelly slumber. As he always did, he slept soundly. And, as it always did, his ability to do so made her jealous. She'd been a light sleeper her entire life and hadn't truly realized how much pleasure a person could derive from a solid night's sleep until she'd met Leo Connelly.

She studied his face by the diffuse light filtering through the bedroom curtains. Always closed and unreadable when he was awake, in sleep, his expression was relaxed and open, as if he'd tell her anything she wanted to know if she could manage to weave her way into his dreams.

If only it were that easy.

He was keeping something from her. That much was obvious. The notion that Ingrid Velder had made a day trip to Pittsburgh to discuss run-of-the-mill budgetary issues was beyond laughable. If the number one person in Connelly's organization had come to see Hank and Connelly in person, it was because whatever she had to say couldn't be put in writing and shouldn't be said over the phone.

Sasha wasn't naïve. She realized those restrictions could apply to at least half of what Connelly did for the government. But she also knew there was no reason for a face-to-face meeting to discuss finances. The logical conclusion was, at best, her husband wasn't being completely forthcoming.

At worst, he was lying to her. She suspected, if she pressed him, he'd say he was doing it to protect her. And because disclosing details to her would be a federal felony.

They'd been together for seven years and married

for five—in no small part thanks to their standing agreement not to pry into the confidences their respective jobs required them to keep. Still, she wondered, and not for the first time, exactly what it was her husband did in the name of national security.

Sometimes—most times—she was glad he couldn't tell her. But other times, like now, that excuse felt a little too convenient. Did they hide behind confidentiality to avoid discussing issues that might drive a wedge between them?

The incessant questions bouncing around her brain made her restless. She stood and crept on silent feet out into the hallway. If she couldn't sleep, she could at least check on Finn and Fiona. To no one's surprise, Maisy had brought them home dirty, delighted, and dead on their feet. They'd fallen asleep within minutes.

She tiptoed over Java, who evidently believed the appropriate place for the family feline to sleep was stretched across the middle of the upstairs hallway. She cracked open the door and peeked into the bedroom the twins shared. The soft glow of the night light revealed they were both sound asleep in their favorite positions—faces down, arms splayed, bottoms sticking up in the air. She eased the door closed, hurdled the cat again, and padded back into her room.

An involuntary glance at the alarm clock on her

bedside elicited a soft groan. It was nearly two o'clock. If she didn't manage to fall asleep soon, it would take an excessive amount of coffee, even by her standards, to drag her out of bed in time for her morning Krav Maga class.

She slipped into bed beside Connelly and tried to still her mind. But she kept returning to the inescapable fact that he was hiding something from her. She pushed the thought aside to focus on the upcoming morning's schedule.

She was making a mental note to bring Naya up to speed on the situation at DoGiveThrive when it hit her: The reason why she was unusually upset about Connelly concealing something from her was that she intended to do the same thing to him.

His pushback when she mentioned Sentinel Solution System's information request had taken her aback. Even accounting for their disparate views on personal liberty versus security, he'd reacted strongly. Unusually strongly. Her instincts told her his behavior meant the NCTC had something to hide. Which, unfortunately, meant she'd soon have something to hide from him.

For starters, if Elizabelle could convince the pastebin site's owner to tell her who had accessed the leaked list, Sasha was certain the company would have grounds to file a complaint against the government contractor. And that was exactly the sort of information she would need to withhold from the man who currently had his right arm thrown across her torso and his face nuzzled in her hair.

She shifted her weight so that her back was pressed against his chest, squeezed her eyes shut, and willed herself to sleep.

6

It was just after one o'clock in the morning local time when the telephone rang in a small concrete structure in a rural community located forty miles east of Houston near the Gulf Coast.

Ordinarily, Fletcher Lee Holden wouldn't have been rattling around the dimly lit interior of the windowless building at that hour of the night. Ordinarily, he'd have been home, snug in bed next to his wife of twenty-five years, Melody Lynn.

But, he reflected tiredly, the past six months had been anything but ordinary. He grabbed the phone, plopped down in the nearest chair, and stretched his long legs out on the surface of the metal desk.

"Hiya."

There was a pause while the caller tried to determine whether Fletcher Lee Holden was really answering the bunker phone in the middle of the night. Fletch went ahead and let him figure it out on his own.

"Mr. Holden? Is that you?"

"Yup."

"Sorry to be calling so late. To tell you the truth, I expected I'd be leavin' a message for someone to pass on in the morning, sir." The caller's voice shook with nerves.

"It must be your lucky night, son. Because you got me. And you are?"

"Oh, sorry. It's me ... Marcus."

Fletch wasn't even sure why he'd asked the man his name. It wasn't like he knew all two hundred members of the brotherhood personally. Back in the day, his daddy had. But that was a different time, and a smaller group.

"I assume you're calling for a reason, Marcus. Or is this a social call?"

"No, sir. I'm calling because I got a hit on Essiah Wheaton."

The voice still trembled, but Fletch could tell it was from excitement now, not nerves.

"Wheaton?"

"Yes, sir. My oldest boy, he's in college up in Georgia. He was doing some recruiting, trying to get a new chapter going. He got to talking about his chapter back home and, well, I guess Wheaton was on his mind. He did a search on the Internet and found the sonofabitch."

Fletch shook his head from side to side. "Wait, now. Didn't we have the webmaster do that back in the fall?"

"Yeah, and he didn't find nothing. I don't know where Wheaton was hiding then, but he's popped out of his hole now."

"Well, where is he?"

"Mars."

Fletch fisted his hand and slammed it down on the desk. The nerves along the side of his hand sang with pain. He spat out from between clenched teeth. "Listen here, it's late. And I'm tired. I don't have time for games. Your son must be doing some pretty strong drugs if he thinks Essiah Wheaton's on Mars."

"Mars, Pennsylvania. It's a town near Pittsburgh, my kid says."

"Oh .... What's the address?"

"Haven't found that yet. That's why I'm callin'. Finding Wheaton was top priority last year. Is it still?"

"Yes."

Marcus paused. Then, "You want me to go up there? See if I can find the guy?"

Fletch weighed the decision for all of ten seconds. "Hell, yes."

"Consider it done, sir."

"Now, Marcus, first thing in the morning, you call Chuck Webster. He's in charge of all security issues. Make arrangements to go up there together. And you two keep me in the loop, hear? Chuck has my cell phone number. Call me direct as soon as you find that weasel."

"Yes, sir."

"You tell your boy good work. And if you help us bring Wheaton to justice, we won't forget it, Marcus."

"No, sir. Good night," Marcus sputtered.

Fletch hung up the phone, wide awake and buzzing with adrenaline. He rolled out the bottom right desk drawer and removed a three-quarters full bottle of bourbon and a paper cup. He poured himself a small drink. Then he raised the cup in a silent toast.

Essiah Wheaton. He'd thought the man was gone for good. If he could find Wheaton, he'd be able to tie up a whole pack of loose ends that had been weighing on his mind something awful.

He tilted his head back and let the sweet burn of the liquid cascade down his throat in one long swallow.

7

Leo and Hank claimed their usual bench at the playground. It was set off some distance from the other benches clustered around the tot lot, which meant they could have their conversation out of earshot of the mommy groups enjoying organized play dates and the nannies and au pairs chatting while they tended their charges. Now that spring had finally sprung, the park was getting crowded enough that they'd need to be discreet.

Hank's kids, older and more self-sufficient than the twins, had scattered to all corners as soon as they'd arrived. Finn and Fiona had plopped down in the middle of the giant sandbox with an assortment of digging and building tools. Leo figured that would give him and Hank twenty minutes or so to talk before he needed to push Finn on the swings or spot Fiona while she scrambled over the monkey bars.

"So, what's going on?"

Hank sipped his coffee from his World's Best Dad to-go mug before answering. "I got a call from Ingrid this morning."

Leo shifted his gaze from the sandbox and studied the side of Hank's face. His expression gave nothing away, but Leo could see the tension in Hank's profile.

"Already? About Storm Chaser?"

"Yes. Or, at least, I suspect it is."

"You suspect? What's that even mean, Hank?"

He sighed heavily. "I don't know. It was an unusual call. She asked me if I was in a secure location. I told her I was, and she gave me a name and an address and told me to have you check out the target. Then she hung up."

The *target*. Not the suspect, not the person of interest. A target could be one of two things. One was the target of an investigation; typically, a United States citizen suspected of being involved in some criminal activity. The other was an actual target. Someone who'd been marked for elimination.

It would be rare, verging on unheard of, for Hank and him to have any involvement with the second type of target. That was the CIA's area—foreign actors, mainly. But Ingrid's demeanor, and the cryptic statements she'd made yesterday, certainly tilted the scales toward liquidation, not investigation. But why?

"Who is this person?"

Hank shifted his weight and raised a hand to shield his eyes from the bright morning sun. Leo followed his gaze to the broad-limbed oak tree, where Hank's youngest girl, Calla, sat with her sneakers propped against the vee formed by two low branches and urged one of her brothers to join her.

For a moment, Leo thought he wasn't going to get an answer to the question.

Then Hank spoke in a heavy voice, "I'm not sure exactly. I asked around some and I heard—not from Ingrid, of course—that a whole mess of names are being fed into the databases and flagged. Any and all hits are being forwarded to a top-secret, interagency effort being run by a joint terrorism task force."

"So this guy, or woman—"

"It's a guy. Essiah Wheaton. The address is some farmette out in Butler County."

"Okay, so Wheaton's a suspected terrorist?"

"Nobody's said that straight out. But nobody's said he isn't."

"Hell, Hank. What am I supposed to do? Walk up to his door and shoot him on sight? Tail him? Interview him? I need something to go on."

They sat in mutual silence. Finn buried a small wooden horse under a mound of sand for Fiona to dig up. Then he did it again. Beside him, Leo could feel Hank seething with frustration.

Finally, Hank spoke. "Don't engage him. Just observe and report back to me. If nobody's going to tell us what we're wading into, we'll have to do our own due diligence. Can Sasha's folks watch the twins or do you want me to take them?"

He shook his head. "Thanks, but her mom's all lined up for grandma duty this afternoon."

Hank clamped a heavy hand on Leo's shoulder. "I'll keep poking around. Wear a vest. Just in case."

8

Leo crouched and peered out from among the Rose-of-Sharon bushes bordering the western edge of Wheaton's property. The hibiscus shrubs were convenient for his purposes, but it was unclear to him what privacy purpose the dense screen of bushes served. The nearest neighbor's home was nearly half a mile away. He'd seen it when he'd parked the SUV on a small dirt road out of sight from the main highway.

Wheaton's house was set back from the road near the crest of a rolling hill that dominated the front yard. Leo looked up at the structure. Two stories plus an attic, brown shingles, and a wide brick chimney. Tidy and well kept. More flowering bushes had been planted on both sides of the house. The rows flanked the front porch, wrapped around the sides, and continued until they were out of Leo's line of sight. The bushes obscured the first floor windows. Someone living inside was either a horticulture enthusiast or a privacy freak. Possibly both.

He saw no signs of movement from within the house, and there were no cars or trucks parked in the long gravel driveway. The driveway continued past the house, circled behind it, and terminated at a detached wooden garage with a wide white door. Judging by the weathered red paint that matched the old barn at the southwest corner of the property, he surmised that it may have once stored farm equipment.

He stood and cracked his back, stiff from the awkward position. He considered whether he was getting too old for surveillance and dismissed the thought. The dampness was just seeping into his bones from the light rain the night before, that was all. Maybe he'd have to join Sasha at her yoga class.

Still trying to work the knots out of his shoulders and back, he skirted the edge of the property, careful to stay behind the bushes to conceal his movement from anyone who might be watching from inside the silent, closed-up house.

He followed the privacy bushes along the perimeter until he was directly behind the garage. His suspicion that the structure had, at one time, been used to house a tractor or threshing equipment was confirmed by a wide doorway that opened to the back of the property. It had no door, but someone had boarded over the opening with two sheets of plywood that formed a crooked X. The loose plywood boards were sufficient to keep out would-be thieves—assuming they weren't terribly motivated—but they provided no protection from prying eyes.

He crept over to the opening, pressed himself against the outside wall, and squinted into the interior. His eyes adjusted to the semi-darkness quickly. A mostly clean, white pickup truck with a Texas license plate was parked on the right side of the garage. He noted the license plate number and continued his inspection. To the left of the truck, there was an empty space large enough to fit a second car—a mid-sized sedan, or possibly a small station wagon.

The only other contents of the sparse garage were a cluster of gardening tools and lawn implements stacked in the far right corner and a riding lawnmower covered with a thin layer of dust. There was a long workbench with a peg board hanging over it. Both the board and bench were empty. There was no hint of any unsavory hobbies Wheaton might engage in—no bomb-making supplies, counterfeiting equipment, or weapons. There was nothing to suggest any savory hobbies, for that matter—not a baseball glove or a set of golf clubs.

He stepped away from the structure with a rising mixture of frustration and puzzlement. As far as he could tell, this information-gathering mission had been a big, fat bust. Nothing about Wheaton's set up said bad guy. The property was secluded and remote. But plenty of people lived rural lives—that didn't make them terrorists. Privacy bushes might screen out nosy neighbors, but they would be useless against government agents. At a minimum, Leo would have expected a barbed-wire fence. Any half decent would-be criminal mastermind would supplement with a trip wire or maybe some vicious dogs. His own murdering father had dug punji stick pits to fortify his house, which was built on the edge of a rocky cliff outside a village that made the small town near Wheaton's place look like a sprawling metropolis by comparison. In short, Leo hadn't seen a single thing that might explain why the government cared so much about Essiah Wheaton. The scene felt *wrong.*

His annoyance at being sent on a fool's errand was tempered by his gratitude that the snug vest and Kevlar plates he wore under his loose sweater had been unnecessary. Every constricted breath he took was a reminder that he could have walked into something deadly.

He continued past the garage to walk the rest of the perimeter before hiking back to his car. He suspected Ingrid and Hank would want him to come back at night. As he walked, he visualized how the property would look in the dark and scouted for a good vantage point to set up with night binoculars.

He pushed through a dense cluster of trees. The copse sat on a small rise above the house. He stared down at the back of the house. With a good set of binoculars, he'd be able to look right in the second floor windows from here. This was the spot.

He was halfway through the stand of trees on his way back to the property line when he heard the car engine. He froze and turned his head in the direction of the sound. It was approaching fast and from the south. That made sense. He'd passed a small commercial strip with a grocery store, a pharmacy, and a pizza joint about ten miles down the highway.

He trained his eyes on the rise in the road and waited. A dark gray station wagon rumbled over the hill. He tracked the vehicle, expecting it to speed by Wheaton's property and continue north. Instead, the driver slowed and turned into the driveway. The car drove up the hill and past the house but stopped shy of the garage.

The driver killed the engine, and the wagon's rear

gate lifted open with a slow, automatic motion. A moment later, a tall, sturdy woman stepped out from behind the wheel. Her light brown hair was pulled back in a high ponytail. She wore a light purple t-shirt, faded jeans, and well-worn boots. She hurried around to the back of the car, pulled a pair of gardening gloves from her back pocket and put them on while she walked. Her movements were efficient and quick. She began to unload large bags of soil or mulch from the car, two at a time. She draped the bags across her forearms, carried them to the large garden plot behind the house and dropped them next to a potting bench. Without pausing, she went back for the next load.

Once all the bags were stacked, she wiped her brow with the back of her hand, glanced up at the house, then resumed unloading the car. Leo watched as seedlings, plant food, stakes, a tray of plants, and a watering can piled up on the bench. The woman surveyed her purchase, hands on hips, with a satisfied smile then got back in the car and started the engine. She drove it up to the garage, hopped out, raised the bay door, then moved the station wagon inside. A moment later, she emerged from the structure with a leather purse slung over her shoulder, rolled down the garage bay door, and walked down the slight hill to the back of the house.

She mounted the stairs to the wooden deck then let

herself in through the back door—presumably into the kitchen. Leo listened hard enough to hear the door's lock *snick* into place. He heard nothing else, no "honey, I'm home" or male voice calling out in greeting.

He turned back to the garage, now holding one truck and one car. There wasn't enough room for a third car. He shook his head. More mysteries. Who was the woman gardener? And, if Wheaton wasn't home, where was he—and how'd he get there?

He trudged the half mile back to his own vehicle, parked on the access road, lost in thought. He walked along the shoulder of the highway, following a berm that had been taken over by weeds and wildflowers. Not a single car or truck whizzed by him. When he was about two hundred yards from the rutted road where he'd parked, a single large red and black motorcycle roared toward him from the opposite direction. The bike's highly polished chrome caught the sun like a flare. Leo raised a hand. The motorcyclist wore a black helmet with a tinted visor. He nodded his head to return the greeting and sped by, kicking up dust.

Leo turned to watch the motorcycle shrink in the distance and caught a flash of a blue license plate with a large white star. *Texas. One question answered.*

Essiah Wheaton followed the bend in the road and disappeared. Leo kept walking.

9

Sasha leaned back in her wrought-iron chair, glanced around the crêperie's cute outdoor patio, and pulled her sweater around her shoulders. It was a bit early in the season for dining al fresco. But the winter had dragged on and on, and everybody was eager for some fresh air and sunshine, so here they were.

She broke off another piece of the chocolate and fruit crêpe she, Will, and Naya were sharing for dessert and forked it into her mouth.

She had to hand it to Will. His latest work-life balance suggestion was genius. He'd proposed a new format for their partners' lunches. They chatted during their main meal without addressing any of the day-today concerns that faced their law firm and left the business matters to be handled over dessert and coffee.

So far, the compromise seems to be working. Sasha had devoured her mushroom and goat cheese crêpe without once thinking of billable hours, accounts payable, receivables, or vendor issues. Talking about their families and current events instead made the actual meal seem like more of a break from work. And administrative minutiae was always more palatable when paired with sweets and good coffee. As a bonus, the discussions were shorter now and sometimes even focused on the substance of their work for clients.

As if Will had read her thoughts and decided it was time to pay the piper, he dabbed an imaginary trace of stray melted chocolate and whipped cream from his lips, folded his linen napkin into a perfect square, and placed it on the table in front of him.

"Shall we?"

Naya nodded her agreement around a mouthful of the crêpe.

Sasha took a sip of her hot, robust coffee and traced the rim of her mug with her index finger. "I'll start us off. I assume Naya told you about my new matter for one of her clients?"

"Yes. This would be the nonprofit fundraising organization that fell victim to a data hack?"

"Actually—" Sasha and Naya began in unison.

Naya laughed and waved her hand at Sasha. "You go ahead and tell it. I'll take care of the rest of this crêpe."

"Nice division of labor. Anyway, they weren't hacked, they were breached. The difference being the data wasn't accessed by an outsider. Instead, a rogue employee posted it publicly just before quitting with no notice."

Will frowned. "Rogue employee may be a bit mild. That's reckless, bordering on criminal."

"I don't disagree. I met with DoGiveThrive's CEO and programmer yesterday. They seem to think this leaker, Asher Morgan, was motivated to disclose the information because he disagreed with a management decision not to respond to an information request from the government."

As she anticipated, Will's white-collar criminal defense lawyer ears perked up at the mention of a governmental information request. "Who issued the subpoena? FBI? NSA? Wait—DoD, DHS? No, ICE?"

"Hang on, did you have alphabet soup for lunch? I could've sworn you ordered the chicken and vegetable crêpe?" Naya cracked, eliciting a rueful chuckle from Will.

"Point taken. I got a bit carried away. My apologies. Please, go on, Sasha."

"Apparently it was none of the above. The request—which was not a subpoena, but an informal request—came from a government contractor on behalf of the NCTC. Oh, and then, the leaker went to work for that very same contractor. The whole mess stinks like a dirty diaper."

She paused to check her partners' expressions for signs of familiarity with the initials. Seeing none she continued, "The NCTC is the National Counterterrorism Center. I poked around on the internet. Apparently, the NCTC evolved after the 9/11 terror attacks. It's an electronic information clearinghouse for all the agencies Will rattled off—and loads more. They work with the National Joint Terrorism Task Force and local JTTFs. They maintain an enormous database of information about terror suspects and upstanding citizens who just happened to have had an overlapping hotel stay or been on the same flight as someone who was flagged."

"Come on, now. Their powers can't be that broad," Naya protested.

Will drew his eyebrows together in a worried vee. "I don't know, Naya ... matters of homeland security get a lot of deference ..."

Sasha plowed on. "I'm sure you both know my views on the matter. In any event, DoGiveThrive's got a solid response plan in place. The CEO is calling every user personally to explain what happened, apologize, and hear their response. Transparency, apology, empathy. It's the best they can do for now."

Naya nodded her approval. "Do you think they'll be sued?"

"Maybe. If they are, I think they get out through motions practice. I don't see a trial in their future. But they might want to sue the contractor. They've got standing. I mean, no matter how well they handle the situation, their reputation will take a hit."

Now Naya's frown matched Will's. "I don't know, Mac. That seems risky."

"Risky how?"

She'd directed the question to Naya, but Will answered. "Risky in that a nonprofit charitable crowdfunding startup operating on a shoestring budget may not want to tangle with a vast government spying apparatus that will surely defend its actions by noting its compelling interest in protecting the country from a horrific terror attack, say?"

She fixed him with a cool stare for a moment then turned to give Naya the same look. "Are you two serious? You'd have one of our clients roll over and play dead just because some puffed-up task force agent with an inflated sense of purpose decided getting his or her hands on a private list of American citizens' charitable giving records outweighed our constitutional rights? Is that really what you're saying here?"

Naya and Will exchanged a look but neither of them spoke.

"I didn't think so."

Their cheerful waitress appeared with their bill and Sasha bit back the rest of her speech. Naya pulled out her corporate credit card to cover the tab. Sasha picked up her coffee to finish it even though caffeine was the last thing she needed. Her heart was racing and her hands were shaking as it was.

The waitress returned with the receipt for Naya's signature.

Will, the consummate smoother of ruffled feathers, leaned toward Sasha. "We needn't hash this out right now, you know. There's no actual evidence the government contractor even accessed the data, is there?"

She pursed her lips a second then conceded the point. "That's true."

Naya looked up and aimed the pen at Sasha. "Just be careful, Mac. You don't want to get in over your head."

"When am I not in over my head?" She waited until their laughter died and continued, "Seriously, though. I hear what you two are saying. Don't worry, I'm not going to do anything that gets me arrested–"

"Again."

She raised an eyebrow at Naya's interjection. "Fine, again. But the idea that some shadowy task force with no apparent accountability or transparency is entitled to the personal information of law-abiding citizens has to stick in your craw, too."

Will piped up. "Of course it does. We're simply suggesting there's no requirement you slay every dragon in your path. Represent your client zealously? Sure. Pick a fight with someone who has the resources to destroy you? Maybe not."

She read the concern in both sets of eyes. "I get it. Promise."

Naya's shoulders relaxed, and Will gave Sasha a relieved smile.

She decided to change the subject to something less controversial. "Did you pick a new e-Discovery vendor?"

"Do you really want to get him started?"

"As a matter of fact, I have a candidate for the partnership to vote on. I've studied the proposals from the four leading contenders and created a spreadsheet comparing the—"

"I move for a vote on Will's proposed candidate," Sasha said in a hurry before Naya sprained an eyeball rolling her eyes.

"Seconded. All those in favor of giving the contract to the vendor Will likes say 'Aye.'"

"Aye," Sasha and Naya chorused.

He frowned. "You don't even know the name."

"Two votes in favor, Will. Or is it three?"

He narrowed his eyes. "Don't you want to see the chart?"

"Why? We trust you. Besides, Naya or I would have just gone with whichever vendor was cheapest."

"Or offered us the best free snacks," Naya added. "You didn't do that, right? You picked a good one?"

"Of course."

"Great. Meeting adjourned." She closed the bill folder and picked up her purse.

Will shook his head and pushed back his chair.

They were walking across the cobblestone patio when Sasha's mobile phone chirped to life. She plucked it out of her bag and glanced at the display.

"That's Gella calling with an update. I need to take this. Go ahead without me. I'll see you back at the office."

They nodded their goodbyes and walked on. She deposited herself on the wrought-iron bench positioned near the outdoor hostess station. The lunch rush was over, and the spot would be relatively quiet and private.

"Hi, Gella."

Gella's voice had the distinctive echoing quality of someone talking into a speakerphone in a mostly empty conference room. "Sasha, I have Elizabelle with me."

"Hi Sasha," Elizabelle chimed in.

"How's it going?"

"We've got an update for you."

"Great. Before I forget, did you happen to review the proposed press release I sent over last night?"

"I thought it was spot on. I signed off on it and forwarded it to our media team."

Sasha smiled. One of the treasures of the legal world was a proactive, responsive client. She could lawyer her stilettos off, but the inescapable fact was that successful management of any matter rested on a client's willingness to execute on her advice.

"Fantastic. So what've you got for me?"

"I have now spoken to—or left telephone messages for—more than eighty percent of our tribe members. By the end of the day, I suspect I'll have reached everyone. Most people have been remarkably understanding, although they're understandably concerned about any potential fallout."

"We can revisit offering credit monitoring if you like. But, again, it seems unlikely verging on impossible that anyone would be able to steal an identity or engage in credit card fraud based solely on a name and a zip code."

"I agree, of course. I've asked Josh, our finance director, to price out the cost of doing so, anyway. It may be worth providing monitoring as a gesture of goodwill."

"Sure. And there's no harm in doing it. That's a business decision you all should make internally. Elizabelle, do you have anything new?"

"I heard back from Paul at the pastebin site. He confirmed the information was accessed and downloaded overnight on Sunday."

Sasha waited, but Elizabelle didn't elaborate.

"How many times?"

The programmer sighed. "Six."

Sasha felt her shoulders sag slightly. Six was better than six thousand, but she'd been hoping Paul would report just one download and would helpfully identify the source as Sentinel Solution Systems. A girl could dream.

"That's not ideal, but it's not *that* bad, right?" Gella interjected, eager for reassurance.

"It could certainly be a whole lot worse," Sasha agreed. "It'd be helpful to know who those six people are, of course. Even assuming one of the downloads was the work of Sentinel Solution Systems, that leaves five unknowns. They could be nothing—kids messing around or even bad guys trolling for information, but who looked at it and realized it's worthless to them. Or, one of those hits could be an enraged ex-spouse, a bitter former business partner, an estranged sibling. It could be anyone unless Paul tells us. You two are more aware of the possible dangers than I am, I'm sure."

On the other end of the phone, Gella and Elizabelle murmured their understanding.

She pressed on. "That's why it's so important to get the names from the site. Did this Paul seem amenable to sharing that without a subpoena or a formal document request?"

"Not exactly, and I get it. He's in a tricky spot. Just like we didn't want to give up information about our tribe members voluntarily, he needs to protect his community members' identities," Elizabelle answered.

"Sure."

Elizabelle continued, "So, while he wouldn't tell me who downloaded the information, he did share the general locations of the internet service providers and devices tied to the downloads."

Sasha smiled to herself. Getting the locations of the ISPs was frankly more information than she'd hoped for at this juncture. "Nicely done. And?"

"The first hit came from Crystal City, Virginia. That had to be Sentinel."

"How sure are you?"

Elizabelle answered immediately, "I'm positive. But I can't prove it."

"It might not satisfy a judge," Sasha agreed, "but for our purposes, we'll operate under the assumption that it was. What about the others?"

"Right before we called you, I was explaining to Gella that two of the hits came from ISPs registered abroad. One in Argentina; one in Germany. This is pure speculation, but if I had to guess, I'd say they were just random surfers who stumbled on the names."

"Before we called you, Elizabelle and I searched our tribe database and confirmed that we have no tribe members in either of those countries. Because our charitable exemption only applies to U.S. taxpayers, we have exceedingly few foreign members. The handful we do have are American ex-patriots, mainly living in Canada and Mexico," Gella explained.

"Are there any international recipients?"

"Again, given our charitable status and the size of our company, right now our footprint is domestic. We did work with some folks in Puerto Rico in the aftermath of hurricane Maria, but that's the only time we've operated outside the continental United States. We simply don't have the resources at this point to send our charity sherpas abroad to do their vetting. Even Puerto

Rico was a strain on the budget, but the island was decimated. And we couldn't just stand by and watch fellow Americans suffer."

Sasha cut her off before she got too far afield. "Okay, that all makes sense. So we've got two foreign hits that, for now, we'll put in the 'likely harmless' category. We've got one hit that we're tentatively identifying as being from Sentinel. What about the other three?"

The sound of papers rustling preceded Elizabelle's answer. "There were two hits from within the District of Columbia, and one hit from a university address in Athens, Georgia."

Sasha thought. "Did the hits from DC come after the one from Northern Virginia?"

"Yes. Paul listed them in the order in which they happened. So it would've been Virginia, DC, DC, Argentina, Georgia, and finally Germany."

"Okay, it seems logical that Sentinel found the data and probably alerted … what, fellow contractors or government agencies?"

"Or their own employees who may have accessed the information from their home computers. It was late on Sunday night," Elizabelle pointed out.

"Excellent point. For now, we'll group those three hits together—they're almost certainly connected somehow. We agree the international hits are likely not a high risk. What do we make of the one from Georgia?" Sasha mused.

Elizabelle whispered something to Gella.

After a moment, Gella said, "We're not sure what to make of it. My instinct is it was probably just a college student hoping to stumble on something juicy like leaked military secrets or some politician's personal emails. Elizabelle tells me that college students make up a significant portion of the non-programmer user base of sites like these."

"That makes sense."

"I was just telling Gella that my only hesitation is Georgia isn't exactly a hotbed of activity. Most of the college students who are active in the programmer community tend be from math- and science-centered schools, particularly in California and the Northeast," Elizabelle explained.

"But it's not unheard of for a student from the Midwest or the Southeast or wherever to pop up, right?"

"That's right."

"If we pressed him harder, do you think Paul would give us any additional details?"

"He might," Elizabelle allowed. "If a lawyer asked him. I think I've gotten as far as I'm going to get without agreeing to go on a date with him. Which ... I love my job and all, but, sorry, not happening."

"Understood."

Sasha was adding 'draft nastygram to Paul' to her mental to-do list when Gella chimed in again and ruined her day. "There's one more thing. Elizabelle decided to check the list of names Sentinel sent against our tribe membership."

"And?"

"There's a match."

10

Leo returned to his vehicle and took out his phone to text Hank an update:

Visual survey of residence yielded little.
Following up on a hunch.
Will call when back in Pgh.

He pulled off his sweater and freed himself from the Kevlar vest. After stretching his arms over his head, he exhaled then filled his lungs again, enjoying the ability to breathe deeply. He stowed the body armor in the SUV's storage compartment, under a quilted picnic blanket and the pool bag filled with life preservers, plastic toys, and beach towels. Apparently, Sasha'd used his car to take the twins to their most recent swimming lesson.

He tugged the sweater down over his head and smoothed it along his torso. He was about to lower the gate and close up the rear when he caught a glimpse of his reflection and reconsidered.

Just maybe, strolling into a biker bar wearing a button-down dress shirt, an argyle-patterned v-neck sweater, and khakis was a questionable decision. He took the sweater off again and draped it over the swim bag. He unbuttoned a few buttons, untucked his shirt, and rolled up his sleeves. He dug around the storage compartment and found a Steelers baseball cap. He put it on and pulled the bill low over his forehead. There wasn't much more he could do about his appearance. With any luck, it no longer screamed 'I'm a federal agent.' Or, at a minimum, it didn't announce it quite so loudly.

He started the engine and headed toward a building he'd noticed while canvassing the area. The long, squat metal-roofed building had caught his attention for three reasons. One, it was unusually large compared to the surrounding structures. Two, it had no windows. In his experience, the absence of windows in a bar meant the proprietors didn't expect glass to withstand the impact from whatever brawls and scuffles that might flare up inside. And, three, there had been nine motorcycles parked in front of it—a surprise, given the early hour.

His pulse ticked up a notch and he tamped down his anticipation. He had no real reason to believe Essiah Wheaton frequented Mugsy's Bar and Grille. He believed the rider with the Texas plates had been Wheaton, but even that was a guess.

Still, the vibration in his breastbone told him he'd learn something at the bar. Trusting in a vibration wasn't the sort of thing he'd ever admit to publicly. But his instincts had kept him alive in the field this long, and he took them seriously.

He kept a close eye on the speedometer, watchful so that his rising excitement didn't result in a speeding ticket and a series of questions he'd need to evade. He passed only a few stray vehicles during the short drive. He slowed and turned into Mugsy's parking lot. The cluster of the motorcycles near the entrance had shrunk, but there were more than a handful.

He circled around to the back of the building and parked near a wide metal door. He didn't expect to be making an emergency exit through the kitchen. But Leo always liked to have options.

Speaking of options ... he removed his Glock from his shoulder holster and turned it over in his right palm, weighing the wisdom of bringing it in with him. He rubbed his jaw with his left hand. Advantage: one never knew when a gun would prove useful in an unknown environment. Disadvantage: walking in with a weapon would inevitably put him in a mindset of scanning for threats, and a person looking for a threat was likely to see one. His mind made up, he unlocked the glove box, stored the handgun inside, and relocked the compartment.

He exited the car and strode around the parking lot to the front door. He squared his shoulders and pushed the door open.

Leo wasn't sure what he expected to find when he stepped inside. But he knew for certain that it wasn't this.

Six metal card tables were spaced a couple feet apart on the gouged and scuffed wooden floor in the center of the room. Two folding chairs were placed across from each table. Two of the tables and their chairs were empty. The other four tables held Scrabble boards. Seven black-leather-clad men and one black-leather-clad woman occupied the chairs. An official Scrabble dictionary rested, open, on the bar.

A handful of spectators lined the bar, frosted mugs in hand, chatting and watching the action. None of players glanced up when the door opened; their eyes were glued to their tiles. But the bartender and two beefy men with long gray ponytails caught his eye and nodded their heads. Part welcome; part 'I'm keeping my eye on you, stranger.'

He nodded back and flashed what Sasha called his most disarming smile. Skirting the activity at the center of the floor, he stepped up to the bar.

The bartender was waiting for him, a bar towel draped over his shoulder. "What'll it be?"

"Any chance I could get a cup of coffee and a glass of ice water?"

"Ice water, I can do. Coffee might take a few minutes —I might need to brew a new pot. These guys have been playing for a while; and some of them like to stay caffeinated during their matches."

The bartender slid a glass of water across the bar and headed to the kitchen to attend to the coffee. Leo sipped the water and turned his attention to the games in progress. The players appeared to be evenly split between beer drinkers and coffee drinkers. Most of the coffee drinkers were leaning over their tile racks and staring at the board like hawks, legs jittering. Some of the beer drinkers, in contrast, were lounging casually in their chairs, as if they were only marginally aware they were in the game. But they weren't fooling anyone. The air in the room crackled as if electrified by all the intense focus.

The bartender returned with an oversized white mug and a handful of creamer cups. "Here's your go-juice."

"Thanks." Leo ignored the half and half and took a sip. It was hot and tasted more or less like coffee. It wouldn't meet Sasha's standards for strength, but it would get the job done.

"So, what's with the Scrabble tournament?" he cocked his head toward the action.

"Eh, that's a monthly thing—the organized tournament, I mean. But there's always something going on here during the day. If it's not Scrabble, they're playing chess or one of the role-playing games. They play cards, too. Oh, they got a book club."

Leo turned his full attention to the bartender. "Really? The same group of guys?"

The barkeep shrugged. "You might've noticed, some of these guys look a little rough. The bikes are loud. And this is a small town. Couple years back, Slim and Ronnie over there signed up for a chess tournament at the library. Let's just say that while their participation was tolerated, they weren't exactly welcome."

Leo nodded his understanding.

The man continued, "They're my regulars. So, I let them do their thing here in the day. I don't get a crowd until happy hour, anyway. It works out for everybody.

They can get together without anybody giving them a hassle. And they buy enough beer and snacks to make it worth my while."

"Don't any of them work?"

Another shrug. "Some of them are retired; some work third shift. There's a couple long-haul truckers who only come around when they're not driving. And, yeah some of the guys have nine-to-fives. They come in on their days off."

Leo surveyed the crowd. "No problems?"

"There's a couple of pricks in every group, you know? But I like most of these guys. I let them store their games and cards in the back." He tossed his head in the direction of the kitchen.

"Really?"

"This building used to house a catering company with lots of employees. There's a bunch of lockers in the back I have no use for. So this crew stows their stuff in the lockers so they don't have to haul it back and forth in their saddlebags."

"So, how many guys would you consider regulars?"

The bartender narrowed his eyes and took a closer look at Leo. "Who wants to know?"

Leo drank his coffee and considered his options. He'd had success in the past saying he was a private investigator trying to track down a beneficiary to let him know he'd inherited money. He figured he could sell that story to this guy, too. But rather than spin a tale on the fly, he might as well stick to partial truths. They'd be easier to remember and likely just as effective.

"I'm just passing through on my way to Pittsburgh, but I have an old friend from Texas who I think moved out this way. He used to ride. I thought he might hang out here. Essiah Wheaton?"

"You just missed him."

The bartender was still studying Leo's face with a careful, calculating expression.

"Oh, that stinks. Any idea where he headed?" He kept his tone casual.

"No."

The bartender turned his shoulder to Leo and started wiping down the beer taps with practiced, efficient motions.

Leo slid a five across the bar and hefted the mug in his hand. He walked down the three steps leading to the sunken dance floor and stood near a cluster of people watching the nearest match. The man the bartender had called Slim placed the word 'aureola' across a double word space, using all seven of the tiles in his rack for a fifty-point bonus.

The spectators whooped, and Slim's opponent cursed into his beer. Slim reached into the tile bag to replenish his rack and grinned. He came up empty-handed and shook the bag upside-down above the table.

"Game over, C.J." He leaned across the table and shook his vanquished foe's hand.

C.J. nodded then called over to the bartender. "Bill, pour Slim a Yuengling and put it on my tab."

"What the devil's an aureola, anyway? Isn't that part of a boob?" the man standing next to Leo said under his breath.

"That's an areola, with no 'u,'" Leo told him.

The guy shot Leo a look.

"My wife nursed our twins. I learned a lot."

That earned him a chuckle. "Well, either way Slim sure dumped a lot of vowels with that one. He's hard to beat."

Slim turned away from his post-game banter with C.J. and acknowledged their conversation. "An aureola's a halo or a nimbus."

"Nice match."

He looked Leo up and down as Bill the bartender pressed a mug into his hand. "Thanks. Do I know you?"

Bill answered before Leo had the chance. "Says he's a friend of Essiah's, just passing through."

Slim gave him another look, a harder one. "You're from Texas?"

"No. I'm not from anywhere, really. We moved around a lot."

The answer, which had the benefit of being true, seemed to satisfy the Scrabble player.

"I hear that." His gaze drifted over Leo's shoulder, as if he was remembering his own childhood.

"I'd like to catch up with him, though. Do any of you guys know where he works or have his number?"

The energy in the room shifted from open to closed, edging toward dangerous. There was a long silence.

Finally, C.J. broke the quiet. "How 'bout you give us your number? We'll make sure Essiah gets it."

Slim nodded his approval of this plan, and the tension eased.

Leo let out a grateful breath then rattled off a dummy telephone number maintained by the agency. To his understanding, anyone who called it would have a mildly confusing conversation with a young woman named Molly, who'd inform the caller that she'd just been assigned this new cell phone number and had no idea what had become of its previous owner.

"You got a name?" Slim pressed while CJ scribbled the digits on a cocktail napkin.

"Chase." It was the first answer that came to mind.

"Okay, Chase. We'll see that he gets the message. Have a safe drive." Bill the bartender inserted himself into the conversation and made it clear that Leo was being invited to leave.

"I appreciate it." Leo nodded, placed his coffee mug on the long railing separating the bar from the dance floor, and strolled out of the bar without a backward glance.

Once the door closed behind him, he stood in the parking lot and exhaled a long whoosh of air. He couldn't shake the feeling that he'd been balancing on a knifepoint during the encounter.

11

Sasha stared at the computer screen in defeated frustration. Essiah Wheaton, whoever he was, had zero recent internet footprint. Which, frankly, seemed more than a little bit impossible. But, aside from some ten-year-old posts about a college football game, the man appeared to be a nonentity. The internet offered up no clues as to why the NCTC was so interested in the man.

She huffed out a breath and stood up. There was only one person who could track down a cipher like Wheaton. And luckily, she worked right down the hall.

She rapped on Naya's door.

"Nobody's home," Naya called from within the office.

"I need a favor."

"Unless you have chocolate, go away."

"I'll get Connelly to bake you brownies ..."

The door swung open.

Naya wagged a finger at her and ushered her inside. "I'm gonna hold you to that. I'm working under a deadline here."

"Does that mean you don't have time to play ghost hunter?"

She tilted her head, already intrigued. Sasha knew she wouldn't be able to resist.

"What's up?"

"You know that list of names Sentinel Solution Systems sent?"

"What about it?"

"Elizabelle ran it against the list of customers that Asher posted online. There was a hit. A guy named Essiah Wheaton."

Naya crossed her arms. "Did you hear one word that Will and I said at lunch?"

"Of course I did," she bristled. "But, look, *you're* the one who asked me to represent these guys. Do you want me to do my job or not?"

"Sure, but—"

"But nothing. The government's interested in this guy for a reason. I need to know what it is so I can adequately assess DoGiveThrive's exposure here. Public information searches come up empty for him.

So you can work your magic and help me or not. It's your call."

Naya stared at her. She stared back, watching as Naya's expression morphed from one of irritation to one of resignation. It didn't take long.

She shoved a pad of sticky notes and a pen at Sasha. "Spell Essiah. Then give me half an hour."

Sasha scrawled the name on the top sheet, peeled it off the pad, and stuck it to Naya's forehead. "You're the best."

"And you're a jerk." Naya plucked the note from her face.

Sasha turned to leave. Halfway through the door, she pivoted back. "Do me a favor and don't mention this to Will just yet."

They locked eyes. Naya frowned. Sasha understood the feeling—it wasn't healthy to keep secrets from one's partner. But, sometimes, sharing could be overrated. They both knew she was going to do what she was going to do, so why waste her time—and Will's—with a lecture she'd ignore?

"Mac, I hope you know what you're doing. And you better tell Leo to make those double chocolate brownies with the caramel drizzle." Naya gave her a gentle push over threshold. Once she was out in the hall, Naya pulled the door closed with a soft click.

12

As Leo piloted the SUV out of town, he organized his thoughts so he could report back on his morning. He zipped onto the highway and headed toward Pittsburgh. Then he initiated a call to Hank through his hands-free set-up.

Hank answered before the second ring. His deep voice filled the interior of the car.

"Find anything?"

"He's tight with a group of motorcyclists."

"A biker gang?"

He considered the question. Could one fairly characterize a group of game enthusiasts as a gang?

"More like a biker book club."

"Excuse me?"

"They have a social club that meets at a dive bar, but

apparently they play board games and cards and read fiction."

Silence.

"Could it be a front?"

Leo lifted his shoulders in a shrug. "It could, I guess. But it if is, they're pretty committed to the charade. I mean, I walked into a Scrabble tournament and watched a guy place *aureola* on the board."

"Nice way to unload a bunch of vowels. Not to mention the fifty-point bonus."

"And he got a double a word score, too. So, while we both know even killers have hobbies, I'm leaning toward this being a group of guys with shared, legal interests."

"Including Wheaton?"

"My questions about Wheaton weren't met with a lot of love. They closed ranks pretty quickly, but they could just be protecting their buddy's privacy."

"Could be ..."

"Or he could be a radicalized terrorist; I know, Hank."

"I didn't say anything," Hank protested.

"No, but you were thinking it—loudly."

They shared a short laugh. They'd worked together long enough that many things, usually the important things, didn't need to be said.

Some people said they were like an old married

couple. Based on his experience, though, they were the opposite of a married couple. At least, when he and Sasha left meaningful things unsaid, disaster usually ensued.

"Leo?" Hank prompted, knocking him out of his reverie.

"Sorry. Obviously, I need to find out more about this guy. Is there any chance we can backdoor our way into the database and see what got him on our radar in the first place?"

Hank huffed, making a noise that was half-sigh, half-snort. "Our marching orders were just to do the leg work. We're supposed to rely on the data analysts' assessment of the information."

"I know."

Hank rolled on as if he hadn't been interrupted. "But, if this assignment is going to turn into a kill order, I'd say we have the right—no, the obligation—to do our own due diligence."

Leo exhaled a breath he hadn't realized he'd been holding. "I agree."

"But we've got to be careful. Don't log in to any of the databases from your laptop. We can't leave any digital fingerprints."

"Then how are we going to access the files?"

Hank was silent.

He palmed the steering wheel and waited another beat until it became clear his boss didn't intend to answer.

Then he cleared his throat, "Are you sure you know what you're doing, Hank?"

"Don't worry. I'm always careful. I'm not going to log in either. When Cole gets home from classes, I'll have him stay with the little ones while I go cash in a favor. Aside from his gaming friends, did you learn anything about Wheaton that would be helpful?"

Leo replayed his morning as if it were a movie. He saw himself skulking around Wheaton's property. Noted the Texas license plate on the truck. Watched as the woman in the station wagon drove up long the driveway and began to unload her plants and gardening supplies. Walked back to the car and spotted Wheaton on the motorcycle.

"A couple things. He's from Texas. He's got a truck and a bike with Texas plates. Grab a pen and I'll give you the plate number for the truck. He's also involved with a woman. Pretty sure she's a Texan, too."

"She couldn't be someone local?"

He hadn't focused on it when he'd seen the woman, but he now knew there was no way she was a native of Western Pennsylvania.

“Not a chance. She’s getting ready to plant her garden.”

“In April?”

“Right. She must not know that there’s guaranteed to be at least one more hard frost before Mother’s Day.”

Hank clicked his tongue in disapproval. “Well, she’s about to find out.”

13

Sasha was deep in thought, reviewing a deposition transcript, when her office door swung open and Naya appeared in the doorway.

She shut down the transcript program and rubbed her hands together. "Well, don't keep me in suspense. What did you find out about our friend Essiah Wheaton?"

Naya pinned her with a dark look but didn't answer.

"What? Is it that bad?"

Naya raked her fingers through her hair then let out a frustrated sound—almost a mew. It reminded Sasha of the noise Java made when he spotted a bird through the kitchen window.

"You didn't find anything?" She said the words

slowly, not quite believing them. Naya had never come up empty on an Internet search—not once in the fifteen years she'd known her. "You're kidding, right?"

"Is this the face of someone who's kidding, Mac? I hit brick wall after brick wall. I've tried every database I can access—not to mention a couple I shouldn't have. This Wheaton guy fell off the face of the earth last year."

"Wait—you did find something, then? Where was he last year?"

When Naya answered, her voice was tight. "He was in a small town in Texas, not too far from the Gulf Coast. But that's all I know. I don't know where he worked, his address, if he has a family, nothing. For all I know, he was just passing through and ended up in the background of this picture that ran in some local newspaper two years ago. Other than that, I came up empty. And before you even ask, yes, I tried calling the *Bendville Gazette*; the number's been disconnected."

She thrust a printout into Sasha's hands. It was a photograph from the East Texas Fall Festival, according to the caption. Behind a row of giant pumpkins lined up for weighing, a handful of festival-goers had been captured as they walked among the displays. Just to the right of a couple holding hands and sharing a bag of kettle corn, there was a young white man, who had his face turned away from the camera and toward a group of men playing horseshoes under a banner spelling out something too small to read. The photograph's caption identified the kettle corn couple as Mandy and Don Sharpe of Bendville and the man to their right as Essiah Wheaton.

"This is more than I could find."

Naya set her mouth in a skeptical frown. "I should've found a lot more than one stinking picture, and we both know it. What's this guy hiding?"

Sasha stared down at the photograph for a moment while Naya's question bumped up against a vague thought that had been floating around her brain. As the two collided, an idea crystallized.

She looked up and tilted her head. "Can you do me a favor and search the rest of the names that were on Sentinel Solution Systems' list?"

"What are you thinking?"

"Maybe *all* these people fell off the face of the earth. Maybe that's why the government's so interested in them."

Naya's eyebrows crawled up her forehead. "Maybe if the government's so interested in them, we shouldn't go poking around."

"Please. Since when do we mind our own business?"

Naya bobbed her head from side to side, acknowledging that she had a valid point. Then she blew out a long breath. "All right. Sure, why not? Email me the list of names."

"Thanks."

"Mmm-hmm. Too bad you can't just log into Leo's laptop tonight and run the names through his system. You'd have your answer in ten seconds."

Sasha laughed. "Yeah, too bad."

Naya left, pulling the door closed behind her. Sasha picked up her phone and dialed Gella's number.

"Yes?"

"It's Sasha. Would Elizabelle be able to tell me which project or projects Essiah Wheaton was involved with—as a donor or a recipient?"

"No, she doesn't have that access. But I do. I'll find out which sherpa was assigned to him and get the details. Do you need this tonight?"

"Tomorrow's fine, thanks."

"Consider it done."

Sasha ended the call and picked up the picture of Wheaton. *What were you up to? And what are you hiding from?*

14

Finn and Fiona were still filling Leo in on their day with Grandma Valentina when the doorbell rang. Leo pressed his forehead against the glass and saw Hank's familiar face peering back at him.

He pulled the door open. "That was fast. I haven't been home but ten minutes."

"I know. I passed your mother-in-law's car at the corner." He stepped inside and grinned at the twins. "Hi, double trouble."

After the cries of 'Uncle Hank' died down, Leo set the kids up with paints and paper at their craft table and ushered Hank into the small sitting room off the dining room.

"I'll be able to see them from here in case they get

the bright idea to paint Mocha again. But we should be able to talk in peace," he explained.

As if the dog had overheard him and remembered his last encounter with primary colors, the chocolate lab came trotting into the room and wedged himself safely between the chairs. Hank chuckled and reached down to scratch Mocha behind the ears.

His laughter faded and his expression grew serious. "Don't ask how I came to know this, because I can't tell you. Got it?"

Leo nodded. "Got it."

"Essiah Wheaton was living in Bendville, Texas, an unincorporated community located about a half an hour east of Houston near the Gulf Coast."

"Never heard of it."

"Yeah, it's a speck on the map. The only reason anyone's heard of it is that it was destroyed by Hurricane Harvey."

"How badly?" A lot of Texas towns had been decimated by the hurricane. The images had dominated the news.

"No, actually destroyed. Apparently, the town, such as it was, is a total loss. The place has been abandoned. The couple hundred people who lived there—Essiah Wheaton, included—scattered."

"Last time I checked, being displaced by a storm isn't a federal crime."

"No. But hunting down and killing Mexican immigrants is."

"Wheaton did that?"

Hank threw up his hands. "Maybe?"

"Maybe?"

"Bendville didn't have a lot going on. No real industry or tourism. It was mainly family farms, a couple small businesses that served the oil companies on the coast."

"Okay."

"What Bendville *did* have was an active, militant white nationalist group. They were sufficiently noisy that they made an internal list of domestic terror organizations."

Leo's gut clenched. "And Wheaton was a member?"

"His name's in the system, Leo. That's all I know."

"What about the woman?"

He shook his head. "I don't know who she is. But I do know this—The Heritage Brotherhood is—or was—no joke. It's not clear if they're still active, but the leader is a dude named Fletcher Lee Holden. Holden's been a suspect in at least four murders. But he's a slippery son-of-a ..."

Leo coughed and jerked his head toward the

kitchen, where Fiona was watching them with wide eyes.

Hank lowered his voice a notch and went on, “We’ve never gotten anything solid on him. If Wheaton was involved with Holden, he was mixed up with some bad people. Can you go back out to his place tonight and poke around some more?”

Leo nodded heavily. “Yeah, after dinner.”

Hank held his gaze for a moment. “If he’s a murderous nationalist....”

“I know.”

Leo looked away. Hank didn’t have to tell him. He’d sworn an oath to protect the country from all enemies, foreign and domestic.

15

Fiona and Finn were playing a game on the kitchen floor that involved two empty boxes, an empty oatmeal canister, and, for reasons that Sasha couldn't fathom, a toothbrush. As long as it wasn't hers (and she'd checked, it wasn't) and they were occupied, she figured she'd leave well enough alone. She was washing the big roasting pan when Connelly and Mocha thundered through the kitchen door, both shaking water out of their hair.

"Hey," she yelped as cold droplets of rain hit her bare neck.

"Sorry," Connelly said as he unleashed Mocha's collar, grabbed the old towel they kept by the door for times like these, and rubbed the dog's fur vigorously. "It started drizzling when we were down on Walnut Street."

"Did he go?"

Mocha was a fair weather walker. He hated to be rained on.

"Yeah, thank goodness. He should be good until morning."

From his spot curled up on the hearth, Java opened one eye. Sasha could've sworn he smirked at the wet dog.

"I'm almost finished up here. Want to help me give the kids their baths in a few?"

Connelly grimaced. "I actually have to go out for a while—it's for … a job."

"Oh." She turned off the water and dried her hands on a tea towel. "At this hour?"

"Yeah, I'm sorry. It's important. You know Hank wouldn't ask if it weren't." He raised his shoulders and gave her an apologetic smile.

She studied his face. He often stayed up late working on his encrypted laptop for Hank, but he generally didn't go out in the field at night. And he never sprang field work on her with no notice.

"Sure. Of course."

She held his gaze for a beat, wondering what would happen if she pressed him on his nighttime task. She dismissed the thought.

He dipped his head and pressed his lips against her

neck. She softened her spine and leaned into him. His arms encircled her waist, and she rested her head on his chest. She almost asked him not to go.

The moment passed.

He pulled back and locked eyes with her. "I'll owe you one. I'll do baths solo on Thursday and you can call one of the girls and go get a glass of wine or two. Deal?"

"Deal."

He crouched on the floor and admired the twins' cardboard creation then kissed the tops of their heads. "Hey, guys, Daddy has to go work. Be extra good for Mommy tonight, okay?"

"Okay," Fiona chirped.

"'Kay, Dada," Finn echoed.

Connelly smiled at them. "I love you, monkey one and monkey two."

"We're not monkeys," Fiona giggled.

"Love you more," Finn asserted.

"Impossible! Wait—is that my toothbrush?"

Sasha buried her face in her hands to hide her laughter.

Connelly reached for the toothbrush then thought better of it. "I'll get a new one."

"Good call."

He shook his head. "Don't wait up. I'll probably be late."

"Drive carefully. The temperature's dropping. The roads might be slick."

"Love you, monkey three."

"Love you more," she called to his back as he hurried out of the room.

He jogged up the stairs and banged around in their bedroom and his office for a few minutes. When he came back downstairs, he headed straight for the door and yelled a goodbye over his shoulder.

Sasha wiped down the counters and set up the coffee for the morning's first pot. Then she clicked off the lights, scooped a twin up in each arm, and balanced them on her hips.

"Bath time," she sang as she marched up the stairs with Mocha on her heels.

The next thirty minutes were a blur. She stripped off the kids' dirty clothes; filled the tub with warm water and all-natural bubble bath; lathered, rinsed, and repeated; then handed over the basket of bath toys and squirters. Mocha gave her a baleful look and trotted out of the bathroom.

He'd learned the hard way that he was an almost irresistible target for their dueling streams of water. Sasha'd learned the hard way that she was, too. Some nights, she entertained the idea of putting on her bathing suit for the water games.

Long after the water had turned cold and the twins' hands and feet had grown pruney and wrinkled, Sasha drained the tub. She bundled Finn and Fiona into the matching hooded towels inscribed with *'Monkey 1'* and *'Monkey 2,'* then carried them, shrieking with laughter, into their bedroom, carrying on a monologue over ever-louder giggles.

"I'll just put these two piles of laundry in the twins' room and fold it tomorrow," she said to no one before dropping them onto their mattresses.

Fiona's head popped out from under her hood. "We're not laundry!"

Finn emerged, cackling, "Momma, you're *silly!*"

She fake-gasped. "Oh my goodness, how did you two get into my laundry?"

After another round of giggles, she got them into their pajamas, guided their chubby hands as they brushed their teeth, then tucked them in. After reading two bedtime stories and telling the next installment in the story she and Connelly had been making up on a nightly basis for months, she saw their eyelids fluttering. She switched off the lamp and the glow-in-the dark stars on the ceiling began to give off their gentle light. She kissed their foreheads and smoothed back their hair.

Fiona was asleep before Sasha reached the doorway.

Finn, as he always did, would stare up at the stars and sing to himself for a few minutes before joining his sister in slumber.

Sasha dragged herself across the hall and collapsed horizontally across the bed, arms outstretched, and closed her eyes. After a long moment, she groaned and sat up to tend to her own bedtime routine. She rustled around in her dresser, searching for clean running clothes to sleep in. Eliminating the extra step of actually getting dressed in the morning was just about the only way to guarantee she made it out the door for a run.

Connelly's government-issued laptop sat atop the dresser. She furrowed her brow. He never left that thing sitting out. She shut the lid and carried the computer across the hall to his office. As she placed it on his desk, she spotted the security fob he used to log in sitting on his blotter. Her hand hovered over the desk for a millisecond as she remembered Naya's joke.

She shook her head and pulled her hand back. She must've been more tired than she realized to even entertain the idea. She pivoted on her heel to leave the room, shaken by the thought that she'd considered trying to access Connelly's private, not to mention top-secret and confidential, files.

As she passed the closet, the door swayed slightly.

She frowned. She made it a point to keep the closet doors securely closed. In part, because Java loved slinking into dark spaces when the doors were left ajar—he had a habit of curling up for a cat nap and getting himself trapped in the pantry, the basement, and various closets. But this closet, of all the closets, shouldn't have been left ajar. This was where Connelly stored his gun safe.

She pushed the door shut with a click then pressed her palm flat against it and paused while an icy finger of worry crawled along her scalp.

Don't snoop.

She brushed away her inner voice's advice, hit the light switch on the wall, and pulled the door open. The gun safe was stowed high on the top shelf. She stretched onto her toes and wiggled her fingers fruitlessly in the air. She came nowhere near reaching the shelf—which, in truth was no surprise. It was at least a foot over her head.

She dragged Connelly's wheeled desk chair across the room and stood on the seat. Her first year torts professor's words rang in her ears as the chair wobbled: *'Did you ever use a shoe as a hammer? A desk chair as a step-stool? Before you judge a plaintiff's contributory negligence, stop and think, who among us hasn't used an everyday item for an unintended purpose? Necessity may be the mother of invention. But invention is the mother of the avoidable accident.'*

She smiled at the memory and steadied herself, bracing her right hand against the shelf as she scooted the safe toward her with her left. She nudged the slim mini-vault to the edge of the shelf, tipped it forward and caught it two-handed as it fell. She hugged the steel box against her chest as she clambered down from the chair with an ungainly, off-balance hop.

She placed it on the floor and knelt beside it. It was small for a gun safe, designed to be portable. It was also keyless. She pressed her index finger down on the biometric pad to be scanned. Connelly had insisted, over her repeated objections, that both their fingerprints be preprogrammed into the security panel. She couldn't imagine what scenario he'd envisioned when he'd dug in his heels, but she suspected it wasn't this one.

Within seconds, a green light flashed, a beep *chirruped* its approval, and the spring-loaded door opened. She peered inside, and her breath caught in her diaphragm. Connelly's heavy Sig Sauer, the gun she'd used to break his nose the night they met, lay nestled in the foam interior. His Glock, however, was missing. She rocked back on her heels and stared out the window into the dark night as the driving rain lashed against the glass.

16

Fletch was at his weekly poker game when the call from Pennsylvania came through.

"Excuse me, fellas. Imma have to take this." He placed his cards face down on the felt, pushed away from the table, and dropped his gold money clip on top of his cards. A couple of guys started bitchin' under their breath, but he paid them no mind.

Business came first, and everybody in his regular game knew it.

"Is it him?" he asked as soon as he stepped out into the hallway near the restrooms and answered the call.

"Oh, it's him all right," Chuck drawled. "And he's shacked up with Karen Leander. At least, that who his gal looks like. It's kinda hard to see through the trees. But, yeah, we found the yellow dog."

Fletch rubbed the bridge of his nose. "Y'all haven't confronted him. Right?"

He briefly closed his eyes while he waited for Chuck's answer. He didn't know Marcus from a hole in the ground, but surely, in the name of all that was good, Chuck hadn't done anything plumb stupid.

"Course not. Jeez, give a guy some credit, Fletch."

"Right. So, what's Wheaton's story? Besides the girl, I mean."

He listened as Chuck and Marcus conferred in low voices on the other end of the phone. After a few moments, Chuck cleared his throat. "He's got a house out in the country. Nothing fancy. A couple acres. It's not fortified or anything like that; it's a good place for a security-minded guy. Up on a hill. Good lines of sight from the house. He'd be hard to sneak up on, if someone had a mind to."

Fletch smiled at the hypothetical. "I hear you. He got a job or anything?"

"Not sure. He's not working at the bank in town. That much I can tell you. We got into town right when it was closing up for the day and watched everyone leave."

In the background, Marcus spoke, urging Chuck to mention some point.

"What's Marcus going on about?"

"He wants me to tell you Wheaton's still got his hog. We saw it in his shed."

It took a moment to realize they were talking about a motorcycle, not a porcine animal.

"You think he's got riding buddies up there?"

"Might have. Haven't seen 'em, if so."

Something about the cadence of Chuck's sentence was off. Fletch didn't know what it was, but he could tell Chuck was holding back information.

Fletcher Lee Holden hadn't clawed his way to his position as Elder Brother of the Heritage Brotherhood by ignoring his gut ... or by shying away from a scuffle.

"Let me talk to Marcus."

"Now, Fletch—"

"Put him on the phone. Now." Fletch lowered his voice to a rough growl.

"Right. Sorry. Hang on."

The card room door swung open, and Denny's head popped out into the hall.

"Fletch, you comin' back or what?"

He didn't answer. Just gave Denny a stone cold stare until he retracted his head like a turtle and yanked the door closed like it was his shell.

"Mr. Holden, sir, it's me, Marcus."

Fletch waited until the man stopped stammering to

take a breath, then he said in a measured voice, "What is Chuck forgetting to tell me?"

"Uh ... sir?"

"I don't have time for this. And I don't like being jerked around. Start talking."

"We haven't seen any friends coming to visit Wheaton or anything like that, just like Chuck said. He's been home all evening, with his woman. It's raining pretty good, so they've been inside most of the night. Looks like they're playing cards. But ... we're not the only ones watching the house."

He waited.

"We saw shoeprints behind the shed or garage or whatever you want to call it. Chuck noticed them."

"Good for Chuck."

Marcus hurried on, his voice a little higher, a little tighter. "Chuck says they were made by men's dress shoes, and they didn't appear to be fresh. But we had a look around anyway. Saw some broken down brush and flattened grass but that was it. Until about an hour or so ago. Right around nine o'clock. Well, maybe a little later. I'm not rightly sure, actually."

Fletch clenched his teeth together to keep himself from exploding. Marcus was hemming and hawing like a punk. Mercifully, Chuck must've wrestled the phone back from him.

"The feds are watching Wheaton, too, Fletcher. An SUV drives by down on the road—that's unusual enough to be noteworthy all by itself. But about ten minutes later, I'm doing a sweep of the area with my night vision binoculars, and I spot a man walking up the hill just behind this line of trees. He's a big guy, clean cut. He's wearing a black windbreaker, black slacks, black dress shoes. No visible weapon. But he's just creeping along in the pouring rain. He vanishes behind the house for a while and we regain visuals on him on the far side of the barn structure. He's got his own night goggles and he looks like he's hunkered down for a while."

Fletcher's gut seized. He could tell his blood pressure was shooting up by the loud pounding of his pulse in his temple.

"Crap."

"Do you think he's FBI?" Chuck's voice was strained, full of terror.

"Be quiet for a damned minute and let me think."

Chuck fell silent.

Fletcher squeezed his eyes shut and pinched the skin at the bridge of his nose hard enough to clear his mind.

"Okay, find out who this guy is."

"How?"

"Criminy, *you're* the blasted security expert, remember? I dunno, send Marcus down to the road to find the SUV and get the plates. Rifle through his glove box if the guy was a total dumbass and left the vehicle unlocked. Try to get a picture of him with the long-distance lens. Just figure it out."

"Right, okay. Should we …?"

It took a moment for Fletcher to figure out what the unasked question was. When it hit him, he felt like his heart might explode right there in the dirty hallway of Denny's illegal poker room. "What? Kill a federal agent? No, you gold-plated moron. Don't go anywhere near him and for Chrissake, whatever you do, don't let him see you."

"We won't. Got it," Chuck promised in a hurry.

"Good. But when you get a chance, take Wheaton out."

There was silence on the line.

"Did you hear me?"

"Yeah, I heard you. Are you sure about this? Don't you want to find out why he left or … anything?"

"No. Just kill him. If the feds are on to him, we're all exposed. Essiah Wheaton will sing like he's the special guest star at the CMAs and we'll all go down. You, me, all of us. You have to get to him before this FBI guy or whoever he is. Understand?"

Chuck answered in a slow, heavy voice, "I understand." After a long pause, he said, "What about the woman, Karen?"

Fletcher thought. If Wheaton's gal *was* Karen Leander, he wouldn't have told her a blasted thing. Her people were one step removed from hippie communists. And if she was some random skirt he'd picked up, he wouldn't have told her anything in that case either. Wheaton was running from his past. He'd hardly advertise it. And Fletcher didn't want the blood of an innocent white woman on his hands.

"Don't worry about her. Just get rid of Wheaton as fast as you can."

He clicked off his phone and shoved it in his pocket. Then he scrubbed his hands over his face and headed back into the poker hall to distract himself until the iron fist of panic wrapped around his throat eased its grip.

Leo shifted his weight, let the night vision goggles dangle around his neck, and shoved his hands under his windbreaker, wiping them on his shirt in a futile effort to dry them. He was soaked through. Every stitch of clothing from his socks to his undershirt was soggy. His thick hair was drenched with water that had managed to find its way under his hood in steady rivulets.

He was cold and tired and so very bored.

Essiah Wheaton and his lady friend were several hours into what appeared to be a quiet evening at home. They moved around the kitchen from time to time, pouring drinks and grabbing snacks from their pantry and then returned to what appeared to be the world's longest game of rummy.

He exhaled and lifted the glasses to his eyes again. As if they'd heard him, the couple cleaned up the cards from the table and put them back in the deck.

Good. Maybe they'd move on to something more exciting. Something like cleaning some assault rifles or counting big piles of counterfeit money. Even bagging up some street drugs for sale. He wasn't going to be picky.

Wheaton said something over his shoulder as he put the cards away in a tall cabinet. She tossed back her head and laughed, exposing her white throat. Wheaton reached into the cabinet and pulled out ....

Leo leaned forward, holding his breath. He adjusted the magnification on the binoculars and zoomed in on the item in Wheaton's hands. And then he groaned. ... A five-thousand-piece jigsaw puzzle of Hogwarts Castle.

He pushed off his heels and turned his back on the

house. He'd had enough. If Hank—or Ingrid, for that matter, thought he was going to stand out in the rain all night and watch Essiah Wheaton put together a jigsaw puzzle, they were dead wrong.

This guy wasn't a domestic terrorist. He was a game-loving homebody.

He pulled out his cell phone and pressed Hank's contact.

As he tromped through the muddy grass, he waited for the call to connect.

"What've you got?" Hank said by way of greeting.

"A cold, probably. Maybe pneumonia."

There was a pause.

"No activity?"

"Oh, no, there was lots of activity. He played cards. Popped some popcorn. Played some more cards. Ate candy. They're getting ready to start a puzzle now."

"A puzzle? Like, a code, maybe?"

Leo laughed at the hopeful note in Hank's voice. "Uh, no, like a five-thousand piece puzzle of the castle from Harry Potter. The worst thing I can say about this guy is he has lousy taste in beer. He's into that hoppy IPA stuff."

Hank refused to be derailed. "Are you sure he didn't make you? Maybe he's putting on a show for you."

"Please. This guy is just living his life. And, of course he didn't make me."

A twig cracked somewhere to his left. The sound echoed in the quiet night like a shot. Leo froze mid-step, the phone pressed to his ear.

"I don't think the system would flag him as a member of the Heritage Brotherhood if he was just some random dweeb. The algorithms don't make that kind of—"

"Shhh."

Hank fell silent. Leo turned his head in the direction and listened harder, straining to hear through the constant beat of the rain.

There. Someone or something was thrashing through the bush.

"There's something out here. I gotta go," he whispered.

"Probably just a raccoon. Or a deer. Call me when it's safe," Hank said as Leo thumbed off the phone.

He stuck the device back into his pocket and removed the Glock from its holster. He prowled toward the noise, moving at a steady pace. Not fast, not slow. He matched his breathing to his footfalls. Even, measured.

He reached an opening between two bushes and stopped.

The person—or animal—had crashed through these

bushes. He crouched and aimed his flashlight at the muddy ground. Already the rain was washing away the tracks that had been left. And he was no expert tracker. But the indentations looked like footprints to him.

He stood and shone the light in a wide arc but saw no fleeing figures. Heard no vehicle engines springing to life. After several minutes, he turned back to the house.

Maybe Wheaton was a master criminal and the noise had been a diversion to distract him so he and the woman could flee? He trained the glasses on the window.

No, the master criminal and his partner were seated at the table, their heads bent over their puzzle.

Leo holstered his gun, pushed his wet hair off his forehead, and returned to the path.

17

Leo shook his head and gripped the steering wheel tighter.

"It wasn't an animal," he insisted, narrowly resisting the impulse to shout at his boss.

Hank's voice cracked through the SUV's Bluetooth speakers, measured and unconcerned. "Then maybe some teenagers were out looking for a spot to party or canoodle."

"In the middle of a torrential downpour?"

"Love knows no limits, Leo."

"I'm pretty sure that's not what that quote means." He shivered and cranked up the heat. If he couldn't be dry, at least he could be warm.

"I don't know what to tell you. If you didn't see the guy ..."

"I don't like it. Is there any chance another unit could be running a parallel investigation?"

While he waited for Hank's answer, he listened to the rhythmic *shick, shick, shick* of the wipers pushing water off the windshield.

Finally, Hank spoke. "I can't say for sure. The Heritage Brotherhood's alleged activities would put them squarely on the radar of half a dozen agencies, and who knows how many teams and special task forces. Could one or more of them be interested in our boy? Definitely."

"So you think—"

"Let me finish. *If* there's another active mission involving this target, I'm confident Ingrid doesn't know anything about it. She wouldn't keep us in the dark about something like that."

Leo nodded along in silent agreement. Ingrid had always struck him as a straight shooter.

Hank gave a dark laugh and continued, "If nothing else, she'd want to avoid the public relations nightmare of two federal agents accidentally shooting each other in a target's backyard."

"When did you get so cynical?"

"When a kill order landed in my lap," Hank countered.

Another long silence followed. Leo drummed his fingers on the steering wheel.

"So what's the play?"

"I don't know, Leo. I really don't. If you really don't think Wheaton is good for it ...."

"I don't. My gut's telling me he might be hiding something but he's not a killer. Let alone an ideological killer."

"I can't go back to Ingrid with your gut."

"And I can't kill a man I know to be innocent. Correction: I *won't* kill a man I believe to be innocent. I won't do it." The heat in his voice surprised him. But he knew he couldn't assassinate Essiah Wheaton. It wouldn't be a justified kill.

"You know I'll back you on this. But you have to get me something solid."

Hank's words landed like a punch.

"I don't *have* anything solid to give you."

"So, go get something."

Hank ended the call. Leo pounded the steering wheel in frustration. He stared at the blurred lights reflecting off the rain-slicked road ahead as he merged onto Interstate 76. It would be quicker to take the highway home at this hour of night, under these driving conditions than to cut off a handful of miles by following the dark twisting, turning back roads his GPS unit was suggesting.

Besides, highway driving caused him to enter an almost-meditative state. Maybe he could set his mind to work on a way to get Hank the solid evidence he wanted while he made his way home. He took several deep breaths and set his brain to work.

Several miles later, he nearly missed the exit for Interstate 276, which shot straight through the heart of Pittsburgh. As he swerved into the exit lane, he had a better idea.

He checked his mirrors—nobody was out driving on a night like this unless they had to be, so traffic was lighter than light. He yanked the wheel to the left and moved back into the travel lane, continuing south on I-79, headed for the airport.

He parked in the short-term lot and made a note to submit the no-doubt outrageous charge to Hank for reimbursement when he returned. He used the long trip on the people mover to attend to his appearance as best he could. He tousled his hair with his hands then raked his fingers through the still-damp strands so they were standing in spikes. It had to be an improvement over the plastered down, drowned rat look.

He'd left the windbreaker in the car. His shoes still squelched with every step, but his socks were halfway to dry. On a scale of frightening to dashing, he deemed himself presentable. Good enough to charm his way onto an airplane? He'd soon find out.

He presented himself at the ticketing desk and flashed his most winsome smile. The tired agent arched an eyebrow. Not in the mood to be sweet-talked.

"What was your flight number? I'll see if I can rebook you tonight. If not, we're offering hotel vouchers," she said in a monotone.

His smile widened. As he'd hoped, the storms would turn in his favor. Usually, he'd have missed the last flight to Houston, but the lightning and wind had resulted in a ground stop earlier in the evening. He might be able to get on a plane, after all.

"I wasn't booked. But I need to get on the next plane going to Texas."

"Texas is a big state, sir."

"Houston, if possible. But I'm not picky." He grinned again.

Still no mirroring smile from the ticketing agent, but her frown loosened. "That's good to hear, because there are several hundred stranded travelers tonight with very definite ideas about where they want to go, and when. Even if there is a flight out tonight, at best you'll be on the waitlist."

Her fingers flew over the keys. He waited. No reason to play his trump card unless a flight was leaving.

She murmured, her eyes glued to her monitor. "Hmm. There's a nonstop leaving in forty minutes. Wait ... it's full. Let me see about tomorrow morning ..."

He leaned toward the desk and lowered his voice. "Ma'am, I'm a federal agent working for the Department of Homeland Security. And I need to get on that plane."

She pulled her head up fast, eyes alert, all business. "Is there a situation?"

"Not on the flight."

He didn't *say* there was a situation in Houston, but it was fine by him if she thought there was. He flashed his old U.S. Marshal ID at her. Hank and Ingrid had arranged for him to keep it, for occasions just like these. Working for a task force that didn't officially exist was slightly easier with the cover of a department that did exist.

She studied it for a moment then returned to her clacking. "I can get you on in first class. Are you carrying a weapon?"

"Yes."

She hit some more keys and her machine spit out a

boarding pass. She tucked it into a paper jacket and handed it to him with a tentative smile. "You're pre-cleared, and the flight's boarding, Agent Connelly."

He noted her name tag. "Thank you, Jennipher."

She stood a little straighter. "No, thank *you.* For what you do."

He gave her a two-finger salute before he turned and jogged toward the gate.

He did this job for people like Jennipher, who believed in their government and trusted it to protect them while still preserving their rights. And people like Jennipher deserved better than the assassination of their fellow Americans without a damn good reason.

He picked up his pace and ran the rest of the way.

18

Sasha slept fitfully. At three-thirty, she woke up for the third time, parched and hot. She stretched out an arm. Connelly's side of the bed was still empty. The sheets cool and unwrinkled.

She padded to the bathroom. She didn't bother to turn on the light. She poured a glass of water from the sink and drank it in a long gulp. Then she returned to the bedroom, flicked on the ceiling fan, and claimed Connelly's side of the bed.

He could have it back when he came home.

She turned onto her stomach. The rain had slowed to a steady drizzle. She closed her eyes and listened to the sound of its patter on the roof mingling with the slow, low *swish* of the fan's paddles as they rotated lazily through the still air.

Where was he, anyway?

She opened her eyes and flipped onto her back. After a long moment of staring at the ceiling, she sighed and reached to turn on the lamp on her bedside table. She opened the small drawer in the table and removed her phone.

After reading the eightieth article about the disastrous effects of light on the sleep cycle, she'd made a serious effort to shut down her devices two hours before bedtime and never check them during one of her bouts of insomnia.

But, she made an exception when her husband was out running around in the middle of the night in the rain with a gun.

She propped herself up against the headboard and slid her finger across the display. Her notifications showed no missed calls, too many new emails, and one text. She opened the text message.

Something came up. At airport. Plane's taking off in 5. Should be back tomorrow. Will call when I can. Love you.

She stared at the phone. Her throat tightened and her pulse fluttered. The text had come in just before midnight.

This was all wrong. Connelly didn't go out of town in the middle of the night unannounced. If he had to travel for work, he did all the laundry before he left; stocked the freezer with meals she could defrost; and arranged for someone to take care of the twins and walk the dog while she worked. It was adorable, really. He seemed to think the household would fall apart if she were left to her own devices.

She thumbed out a response.

Where are you? What's going on?

The phone vibrated in her hand. A new text had arrived.

On the ground now. Just running an errand for Hank. Go to sleep. I'll see you tomorrow. XOXO.

She gritted her teeth at the non-answer. She considered calling him, but she knew if he answered the call, he wouldn't tell her anything more than he already had. Which was nothing.

Be careful. Love you, too.

She sent the text, switched off the lamp, powered down the phone, and flopped back on the mattress and planned out her morning.

SHE JABBED at Hank's doorbell and depressed the button longer than was strictly necessary.

A moment later, a bleary-eyed Hank pulled the door open and eyed her with sleepy concern.

"Sasha, it's six o'clock. Is something wrong?"

"Uncle Hank!" Beside her, Finn grinned at him. Fiona yawned.

"Nope, nothing's wrong," Sasha chirped. She wriggled out of the backpack filled with food, books, toys, and changes of clothes and shoved it toward Hank one-handed.

He reached for the straps slowly, still processing. She took a sip of coffee from her travel mug and bent to kiss each of the twins in turn.

"Okay, love bugs, be good for Uncle Hank today."

"Okay," Fiona mumbled, still half-asleep.

"We will!" Finn, the morning bird, promised.

She straightened to standing and locked eyes with Hank.

"What's going on?" he asked, drawing his eyebrows into a vee.

"You tell me."

"I don't—"

"My husband left the house last night to do something for you. He didn't tell me where he was going, what he was doing, or when he'd be back. I woke up in the middle of the night to a text telling me that he was on a plane going I don't know where to do I don't know what. He won't give me any answers, so I'm not even going to bother to ask you. But, I have a business to attend to. So I'm going for my morning run, then I'm going to shower and go into the office. You want to send my husband God-knows-where, you can watch my kids." She was shaking with anger but she kept her voice light, pleasant even. She knew the twins were listening to every word.

Hank's littlest one peeked out from behind Hank's bathrobe and clapped her hands with excitement when she saw the twins.

"Finn! Fiona!" Calla raced out onto the porch, took each of them by a hand, and dragged them inside. From within the whirlwind of squeals and laughter, the twins shouted their goodbyes to Sasha.

She smiled at the kids and returned her eyes to Hank's face and let the smile fade.

"Sasha ..."

"What?"

He sighed. "I don't know where Leo is."

She pursed her lips and maintained eye contact.

"I mean. I didn't specifically send him out of town. He's working a very sensitive matter. It's—"

"Save it. It's top secret, confidential, need to know. Everything's secret with you two. Whatever. I have things to do."

She turned to leave.

"Sasha."

She iced him with a look over her shoulder. “What?”

“I’m happy to have the kids for the day. And I’m sorry he left you in a lurch. But you know him better than anyone. He wouldn’t do that to you unless he really *really* had to. And you’re right, I can’t tell you what’s going on. But I can tell you this: He really had to do what he did. You have to have a little faith.” His eyes were serious and more than a little sad.

“Do I, Hank? Do I really?” she shot back.

Then she pushed her hand through the air, dismissing the entire conversation. It wouldn’t get her anywhere. She placed her travel mug on the ledge by Hank’s stairs to retrieve when she came back for the kids and raced down to the sidewalk.

As she ran, Hank’s voice looped through her head, repeating one sentence, the cadence matching the strike of her feet against the pavement:

You know him better than anyone.

Did she, though?

She powered up Forbes Avenue—the steep hill that was Pittsburgh’s answer to the Boston Marathon’s Heartbreak Hill—and had to focus all her attention on pushing herself forward. Her worries about Connelly were pushed out of her mind as she gutted her way up the incline.

When she crested the hill, she took a triumphant

breath as endorphins flooded her nervous system with something akin to joy.

But, as she ran on, her worries returned, chasing her along her route, threatening to overtake her.

Did she really know her husband? Did anyone?

She ran faster, but she couldn't outpace the thoughts that dogged her every step.

19

By seven-thirty, Sasha was ensconced in her office, her third coffee of the morning at her elbow, drafting correspondence. Letters that required responses had piled up for several of her cases. Sometimes it seemed lawyers liked nothing better than exchanging snippy letters. As luck would have it, she was feeling very snippy.

So she plowed through the stack, dashing off terse responses pointing out how incompetent, misguided, or plain old wrong her adversary's position was. And, as was her custom, instead of the typical lawyer closing of 'Regards' or 'Very Truly Yours,' she ended each letter with her favorite valediction, 'All Best.' It made her smile, and that was reason enough to do it. Although she'd once substituted 'Warmest Wishes' in response to a letter whose drafter had warned her in her closing to 'Please Govern Yourself Accordingly,' under the theory that *that* dude needed all the warmth he could get.

She was about three-quarters through her mountain of overdue letters when Naya appeared in her doorway.

"Got a minute?"

She saved her file and nodded. "Sure. Come on in."

Naya pulled the door shut behind her. She gave Sasha a close look. "Everything okay? Caroline said you got in before she did this morning."

"I wanted to get an early start. I needed to catch up on a few things." She waved a hand at the letters on her desk.

Naya narrowed her eyes. "You look tired."

"The storms kept me up last night."

She rarely hid personal stuff from Naya. She was, after all, Sasha's closest friend. Plus, it was a pointless exercise. Naya was as good at reading people as Sasha was. Her friend and partner would know she was lying. But she just wasn't up for a discussion about Connelly's secrecy. Not now.

Naya gave her a skeptical *hmm* but let the subject go—for now. Sasha had no doubt she'd return to it at some point.

"Anyway, you were right about that list from Sentinel

Solution Systems. Every single one of those names is a non-entity as far as the Internet is concerned."

"All of them?"

"All of them. Most of them had a fairly typical digital footprint until sometime last year when they just—*poof*—vanished."

Sasha bit down on her lower lip for a second. "How is that even possible?"

"It's beyond weird. And it can't be a coincidence. But here's the other thing, that fact—that they've gone dark—is the only thing that seems to connect these folks. They're from all over the country, every possible age, gender, race, and ethnicity. I mean, they have nothing else in common."

"It doesn't make any sense."

Naya cocked her head. "Well, maybe it does. It explains why the NCTC is so interested in these people. I mean, they must be hiding for a reason."

"What? If they aren't guilty of this, they must be guilty of something else? Spoken like a true prosecutor."

Naya bristled.

Before they could debate the issue, Sasha's phone rang. She jabbed the intercom button with her index finger.

"Yes?"

"Gella Pinkney's on the line," Caroline told her.

"Put her through."

She hit the speakerphone button. "Hi, Gella. I've got you on speaker because Naya's here. We were just talking about your matter."

"Hello, Naya," Gella greeted her corporate attorney warmly.

"Gella," Naya responded.

The niceties out of the way, Gella got right to business. "I have a list of Essiah Wheaton's donations. He donated to every single fundraiser we posted for hurricane relief in the wake of Harvey, Irma, and Maria. Every one. And, as you might imagine, there were quite a few."

"How many are we talking about?" Naya asked.

"Over three dozen. And he donated between five hundred and a thousand dollars to each one. That's on the very high end for our donors. For a sense of scale, the average donation is thirty dollars."

Sasha had been scribbling notes on the pad she kept by her phone. She put down her pen. "So this guy donated, what, twenty thousand dollars or so? Since when, last fall?"

"That's right. To be precise, he donated twenty-eight thousand dollars. All but a thousand of it to hurricane victims."

Naya and Sasha locked eyes. Sasha knew they were

having the same thought. The donation that broke the pattern would tell them the most about this guy.

"What about the other thousand?"

"Oh, that was to an anti-racism group. He made it right after that ... um ... white separatist march that turned violent back in January."

The march had been billed as a unity rally on a college campus. It had devolved into a riot, leaving two dead and more than a dozen severely injured.

"What was the name of the organization?" Naya asked.

Gella hesitated.

"We need all the information we can get," Sasha urged.

"I know. I just...." She sighed. "It's complicated. This particular group, Standing United, was threatened with a lawsuit by the rally organizers, who claimed their campaign was defamatory. Our charity sherpas stand behind every word of the fundraising request, but Standing United didn't want to feed that narrative, so they removed their fundraising project and credited back the donations. There's a notation in the file that Mr. Wheaton refused the credit."

"That's interesting," Naya offered.

"It is. But it doesn't explain why the counter-terrorism center was so interested in him. He donated to a bunch of hurricane relief projects and an anti-racism campaign. He hardly sounds like a terrorist," Sasha mused.

"I agree wholeheartedly," Gella weighed in.

"Well, this settles it. I recommend we file a complaint against Asher Morgan and Sentinel Solution Systems. Once they get counsel and reach out, we tell them we plan to add the NCTC as a defendant. I trust they'll settle quickly. They obviously were using a bad list."

Naya's lips thinned, a clear sign of her displeasure. Sasha pretended not to notice.

Gella spoke haltingly, "I'll have to talk to my board. But before we even get to that point, there's a complicating factor."

Of course there was. There was always a complicating factor.

"Which is?"

"There are only four people I haven't been able to reach by phone. Mr. Wheaton is one of them."

"So he doesn't know about the breach?"

"He may, but he hasn't heard it from me. He's on my list of follow-up calls to make today. Should I still talk to him?"

'Good question,' Naya mouthed.

It was a good question. And, unfortunately, Sasha didn't have a good answer.

From a legal standpoint, she was inclined to advise Gella not to call him. Of the fifty people on the NCTC contractor's list, he was the only hit. Which meant that of all the names that Asher leaked, Essiah Wheaton had the best claim against DoGiveThrive. Her instinct was to tell her client to lawyer up.

But, from a public relations/crisis management perspective, Essiah Wheaton was a big donor, someone the company needed to keep as a satisfied tribe member. If Gella lost his trust, it would be a blow.

Sasha clinked her pen against her teeth, weighing the two bad options.

Finally, she said, "Definitely call him. Be forthcoming about the leak, but stick to your prepared remarks. We don't know *why* his name was on that list from Sentinel Solution Systems and you can't speculate, so don't mention that part at this point."

Gella made a noise that sounded like a protest, but Sasha went on, "Once we know what the NCTC was looking for, maybe we can share that with him. But we don't know anything concrete right now. And you never take a problem to a client without having a proposed solution ready."

It was Lawyering 101. She figured it would apply equally to online crowdfunding.

"I guess you're right." Gella sounded unconvinced.

"I know I am," she said with more confidence than she felt. "Make it a priority to get ahold of Wheaton today, and then, please call me once you've talked to him."

"Okay. Thank you, ladies."

Sasha ended the call and met Naya's eyes. "What?"

"Are you sure about this, Mac?"

"Do you have a better idea?"

Naya shook her head. "No."

Sasha tried to ignore the way her stomach was flip-flopping. "Well, there you have it. I'm going downstairs for more coffee. You want anything?"

"No, I'm good." Naya trailed her to the door. "Are you going to tell Will that you plan to sue the NCTC?"

"Correction: I plan to *threaten* to sue the NCTC. And I will tell him. But the issue isn't ripe. There's no reason to even bring it up if Gella can't convince her board."

"I hope you know what you're doing, Mac."

As Sasha headed down the hallway in search of a fresh jolt of caffeine, Naya's words rang in her ears like a warning.

I hope so, too, she thought. *I really do.*

20

Bendville, Texas

Leo guided the rental car along the buckled, torn-up road. Large sections of the rural route had been destroyed by flooding in the wake of Hurricane Harvey. The condition of the road had made for a slow trip from Houston to the Gulf Coast town where Essiah Wheaton had once lived.

He was stiff, tired, and hungry. But taking a break to stretch his legs and fill his belly was the furthest thing from his mind. He needed to gather some intelligence about Wheaton and get on an airplane headed back home, and fast. He knew Sasha would be furious with him, and the longer he was gone, the madder she'd be.

Apparently, she'd shown up at Hank's house at the crack of dawn, metaphorical guns blazing, and told him he was her new babysitter. Leo lifted one corner of his mouth in a half-grin at the memory of the picture Hank had texted him: Fiona and his youngest girl had given him a makeover. Complete with sparkly purple nail polish.

His smile faded instantly. Hank hadn't asked any questions about where he was or what he was doing. Plausible deniability was an occupational requirement. But more than that, he suspected Hank didn't want to be put in the position of knowing where Leo was but keeping that information from Sasha.

He needed to focus and make this trip worth the rift that it would cause in his marriage. And the only way to do that was to come back with information that would prove to Hank and Ingrid that Wheaton didn't need to be dealt with through extrajudicial murder.

He took a gulp of water from the bottle provided by the rental car company and frowned at the pile of debris that blocked the road ahead. He cursed and pulled over to what had once been the shoulder of the road. Now it was just a deep rut.

He stepped out of the car to examine the broken

concrete and twisted metal that lay in his path. As he stared at it, he realized it had once been a bridge. The rental car agent's disbelief when he'd told the man his destination was Bendville suddenly made sense.

The man had said, "Bendville's gone. You must be headed to one of the nearby towns."

Hank had said the place had been abandoned in the aftermath of the hurricane, but Leo never imagined it would be completely inaccessible. Just what he needed. A wild goose chase.

He returned to the car and dug out the map he'd taken from the rental counter. He unfolded it and spread it out on the hood of the sub-compact.

He traced a finger along the road he'd taken from the airport. Bendville was about thirty miles ahead. A long walk—too long. Especially if he'd reach a ghost town at the end of his journey.

He tapped his ring finger against the map. His wedding ring made a clinking noise as it hit the hood. There were two nearby towns.

He'd passed the exit for the first about fifteen minutes earlier. From the highway, Sugar Crest had appeared to be a typical, affluent ex-burb. Large white mansions with lush green, manicured lawns rose up on both sides of the ramp from within gated communities. Equally well-maintained golf courses and a large high school complex with a professional-sized football stadium, a cluster of upscale open air malls, and a gleaming hospital were interspersed between and among the developments.

He shook his head. The answers he needed wouldn't be found in a place like Sugar Crest. He felt it in his bones.

He admonished himself, already sure what Hank would say to such a sentiment: *Your bones are no better than your gut.*

He moved his finger and brought it down on the smaller, closer dot. Hyacinth lay just to the east of his current location. He surveyed the flat landscape. In the distance, beyond acres and acres of scrub grass, he spotted a long low brick church with a white obtuse triangle-shaped roof topped by a tall white steeple. Assuming the small town was like most, the church would be on one of the main thoroughfares.

The cross road to Hyacinth was on the far side of the collapsed bridge. The only other option on the map would require a detour back toward the airport, even further than Sugar Crest.

But as he stood here, the church was far fewer than thirty miles away. Definitely walkable.

But he'd spent enough time in the southwest to know there had to be an access road somewhere along this road that would cut through those fields. He refolded the map and returned to the car. He executed a smooth U-turn and crept along the deserted, condemned road for two miles until he found a hard-packed dirt road. He barreled along the road as it snaked through the tall prairie grass, bumping his way toward Hyacinth and answers. A town with a church ought to have a library. Or barring that, a bored cop with a long memory.

HYACINTH, as it happened, had both. In one convenient package.

Leo stopped at the town's lone gas station, bought some more water, a bag of pretzels, and a candy bar, and asked for directions to the town library.

The young guy behind the cash register squinted at him. "Sorry, library's closed Tuesdays through Thursdays."

"Really? Completely closed?"

"Well, yeah. Because the police station's open."

"Okay."

The cashier wasn't making any sense. But, judging by the thick layer of dust on the counter, the gas station didn't get much traffic. Maybe the guy got high to pass the time. Whatever the story was, he clearly wasn't going to have any useful information to offer. Leo scooped up his change and his snacks and turned to leave.

"Wait, don't you want directions to the police station?" the man called after him.

Actually, he did.

"Sure."

"Go to the corner and turn right. It's halfway down the block on your right. Next door to the library. You can't miss it."

"Thanks," he called back in a cheerful voice. Then he pushed the heavy glass door open and hurried out into the parking lot. He found himself wishing Sasha was there so they could laugh together at the weird encounter.

He pulled out, turned right, and, as promised, spotted two twin brick buildings sitting side by side. *Hyacinth Public Library* was emblazoned on the awning over the door of the first building. A closed sign hung in the door's small window with the following note scrawled in marker under the word 'CLOSED': *Return books and DVDs next door when closed.* The neighboring building's awning read *Hyacinth Police Department* in the same font and color. An 'OPEN' sign hung in the window set in its door.

There appeared to be a shared parking lot behind the two buildings, but there was an empty space right in front of the library, so he pulled into it. No meters. He liked Hyacinth already, its odd gas station attendant notwithstanding.

He locked the car and hurried inside. An older, African-American woman with short white hair and perfect posture looked up from a tangle of yarn she was working on and eyed him over a pair of eyeglasses.

“Can I help you, son? Library drop box is over there.” She waved a knitting needle toward a short hallway behind her.

“I’m looking for the chief.”

She placed the knitting on her desk. “You found her. You’ve also found the town librarian and one half of the volunteer fire department.”

He grinned and stuck out a hand. “Ma’am, I’m U.S. Marshal Leo Connelly,” he lied smoothly as he flashed his old ID.

“Violet Lincoln.” Her handshake was firm and brisk. Her eyes searched his face. “A marshal, huh? You don’t mean to tell me we’re harboring a fugitive here in Hyacinth, do you?”

“Not to my knowledge, chief. But I was hoping you could give me some information on a resident—well, a former resident—of Bendville.”

Her eyes dimmed. “I’m afraid all of Bendville’s residents are former. Harvey didn’t leave much behind when he swept through there.” She waved him toward a seat. “I’ll help you if I can.”

“Much obliged.” He hesitated near the chair and swiveled his head around the lobby. “Do you have a gun locker or anything? I’m carrying.”

She waved the question away. “If I stopped what I was doing to lock up every concealed firearm someone carried in here, that’s all I’d get done every day. Just keep it holstered. So, which of Bendville’s fine citizens are you interested in?”

“A guy by the name of Essiah Wheaton. Ever heard of him?”

She pursed her lips. “Yeah. I know Mr. Wheaton.”

“I get the sense you’re not a fan.”

She moved her knitting to the side and propped her feet up on her metal desk. “I’ll be frank, Agent Connelly. Folks around here didn’t shed many tears when that storm swept through Bendville. Now, I know that sounds cold, but lots of people thought Harvey destroying that dang town was God’s wrath.”

“Because of the Heritage Brotherhood?”

She blinked then covered her surprise. “That’s right. Bendville is—was—an unincorporated community. They didn’t have a police force of their own, which meant some of their people viewed obeying the law as an optional activity. The Heritage Brotherhood started out like lots of groups do. A bunch of loud-mouths getting together and spouting off, having rallies, and whatnot. That's their First Amendment right, and more power to them."

"But?"

"But, a fellow by the name of Fletcher Lee Holden rose through the ranks of their little club. And the more powerful Holden grew, the bolder and more violent the Brotherhood grew. By the time that hurricane flattened Bendville and scattered them to the four corners, they were stalking Mexican immigrants, blowing up apartment buildings, and amassing an arsenal that was outsized even by Texas standards. They were bad news."

"How's Wheaton fit in?"

"As I understand it, he was their money man. He was a banker with some online bank. Bendville didn't have a community bank, see. But Wheaton could get the Brotherhood lines of credit, working capital, personal loans through his virtual bank. There was talk that he laundered some money for them, too. I don't know the details."

If Wheaton had been financing the Heritage Brotherhood, the FBI's Financial Crimes Division or the Treasury Department or both would have a file on him. Either one could've sent a team out to Mars.

He snapped his attention back to the police chief. "Did the Heritage Brotherhood survive? Are they still active?"

She made a low noise in her throat. "They've been weakened, for sure. They're spread out, now, and they seem to be keeping a low profile in their new communities. But as long as Holden's around, they're a danger. He's quietly rebuilding them. I have no doubt."

He stood up, thinking. They'd need access to capital to rebuild. So why was their banker holed up in a small town in western Pennsylvania?

"Thanks for the information, Chief Lincoln."

"My pleasure. You run across Essiah Wheaton, do me a favor and aim a kick square to his teeth. Oh, and tell him he has a sizeable outstanding library fine for that DVD collection he lost."

She nodded a goodbye and picked up her skein of yarn as he let himself out of the building.

He suppressed a laugh as he noticed the marker-scrawled message on the reverse of the 'OPEN' sign. Under 'CLOSED,' handwritten letters advised the residents of Hyacinth to *Report crimes and malfunctioning fire alarms next door when closed.* Violet Lincoln was one busy woman.

He mulled over the new information about Wheaton during his short walk.

He was most of the way back to the rental car when his phone buzzed. He fumbled it out of his pocket with one hand while he unlocked the car door with the other.

"I was just about to call you," he told Hank.

"Did you find your exculpatory evidence?"

"Not exactly."

Hank's voice was heavy. "I leaned pretty hard on Ingrid. Your boy Wheaton was mixed up in some plot to kill the Governor of Texas."

"I don't recall an attempt on the governor's life."

"Bad timing—well, good timing, for the governor. The hurricane hit and the Heritage Brotherhood had other priorities—like rowing themselves to safety."

"And Wheaton was part of the plot?"

"He wasn't going to be the shooter or anything, but evidently these bozos engage in the illegal weapons trade to finance their extracurriculars and—"

"Let me guess, Wheaton laundered their money."

There was a loud silence on Hank's end. Finally, "Well, yeah ... what did *you* learn?"

"Essiah Wheaton was—or possibly still is—some kind of internet banker. According to local law enforcement, he handled the Brotherhood's financial matters."

"Are you on your way to the airport?"

"Yes."

"You might as well go straight to Wheaton's and take care of things."

He clenched his jaw. He knew Hank was right. The decision had been made several pay grades above his, and his independent snooping supported the order. But still, killing a U.S. citizen rankled.

"Leo?"

"I'm here. I heard you. I'm just ... thinking."

"You've got until you're back in town to wrestle with your conscience. After that ..."

"I know. I gotta go. I need to make an airline reservation." He heard squealing and giggling in the background at Hank's. "Wait—how are the kids doing?"

"They're having a ball. I'm gonna go out on a limb and say naptime is not happening today."

Leo chuckled, but his stomach felt as if it had been hollowed out. The conversation seemed surreal, as if it were happening in a dream. He was calmly discussing an assassination in the same breath as his kids' nap schedule.

He glanced at his watch. If the flight worked out, he could fly back to Pittsburgh, kill Wheaton, and be home for lunch. He turned the key in the ignition and started the car.

21

Sasha's stomach hurt. *Too much coffee and angst and too little sleep and food. She'd end up with a stomach ulcer at this rate.*

She was reaching for the phone to see if Naya had any interest in an early lunch. It lit up and beeped before she touched it.

"Yes?"

"It's Gella again," Caroline informed her.

"Thanks, put her through."

"Will do. Um, Sasha?"

"Yes."

"Is everything okay?"

She smiled to herself. Caroline, the soul of discretion, sounded so hesitant. Sasha knew what she was asking. Unlike Will or Naya, she very rarely set her phone to 'do not disturb' and let the reception desk field her calls. But, today, she had no desire to speak to Connelly—assuming her wayward husband even planned to call her. So she'd sent her work calls to Caroline's desk and disabled the notifications on her cell phone.

"Yep. I have to get some things done this morning, so I don't want any unnecessary interruptions," she lied.

"Of course. Here's Gella."

"Gella, hi. Did you get in touch with Mr. Wheaton?"

"No, I'm afraid I didn't. I left another voicemail message. But that's not why I'm calling."

"Oh?" Sasha braced herself for the inevitable. If fifteen years of practicing law had taught her anything, it was that clients never called because things were going swimmingly. With precious few exceptions, all news was bad news.

"I've got good news."

"Really?" Maybe she should consider a specialty in representing charitable organizations.

"Yes. The board voted unanimously to authorize litigation against Asher Morgan and his new employer. The directors agree that taking swift, decisive action against Asher and Sentinel Solution Systems will show how very seriously we're taking this privacy breach. How quickly can you file a complaint?"

She calculated, letting the dream of lunch slip through her fingers like a balloon tied to a ribbon. She could draft a serviceable complaint by the end of the day. But she couldn't pull an all-nighter finalizing it. She had a hunch Hank didn't offer overnight child care. And who knew when Connelly planned to grace his family with his presence?

"I'll have a draft for you to review later this evening. We'll file electronically, so assuming you don't have a lot of comments, it could be docketed before lunchtime tomorrow."

"That's perfect. I'll clear my schedule and will be available all evening."

"Did you and the board discuss the possibility of naming the NCTC as a defendant, depending on how the facts shake out?"

"We did. And it's something we'll need to give careful consideration to at a later time with the benefit of more information."

"That seems sensible. I should get started."

"I'll call if I have any luck with Mr. Wheaton."

"Great." Sasha hung up, her hunger forgotten, the mess with Connelly forgotten.

The familiar buzz of hyperfocus and adrenaline was already building in her veins. She closed her eyes to center herself, cranked up her music, grabbed a legal pad from the stack on her shelf, and started writing. Twenty minutes later she had a list of research questions she needed to answer before she started writing the complaint.

She stood, stretched her back, and peeked out into the hallway.

"Psst, Jordana."

The firm's part-time intern wheeled around at the sound of the loud whisper.

"Hey, Sasha."

"Hi. Could you do me a huge favor and run down to Jake's and get me a refill, please?" She shot the girl a high-voltage smile, pushed the door open another couple inches, and thrust her mug out.

"No problem."

"Awesome, thanks." She pulled the door most of the way closed and returned to her desk.

By the time Jordana returned with a fresh coffee, she'd plowed through her list of research issues.

The girl placed the mug on the desk near Sasha's left elbow and put a package of Jake's homemade granola and a container of yogurt next to it.

"Thanks, but you didn't need to get anything to eat."

"Um ... you look really busy."

Sasha opened her desk drawer and removed a spoon.

She ripped off the lid to the yogurt and dumped the granola on top. As she stirred it up, she said, "I am. I need to draft a complaint by the end of the day. But it's not your job to feed me."

She held the spoon in her mouth and reached for her wallet.

Jordana shook her head. "No, it's okay."

"Jordana, I'm not letting you pay for my food."

"I didn't. Caroline said whenever it looks like you might work through lunch, we should get some money out of petty cash and buy you a high-protein, moderate fat snack that you can eat easily ... otherwise you get cranky." She shifted her weight. "Sorry."

Sasha scooped out the last of the yogurt and swallowed it before responding. "Caroline's a perceptive woman. Thanks for the coffee *and* the snack."

Jordana exhaled and laughed at the same time. "Oh, wow. I was afraid you might get mad." She loosened her shoulders and leaned over to peer at Sasha's laptop screen. "You're doing legal research, right?"

"I just finished, actually." She doubled-checked the items on her list. Yep, each entry had a line drawn through it.

"How'd you do it so *fast?*"

She laughed. "The magic of computers. When I started practicing, we still used physical books to do research—there were rows and rows of digests in this enormous library at Prescott & Talbott. Research took ages."

"That can't be right. Didn't you graduate from law school in 2003 or something?" She shot Sasha a skeptical look.

"Oh, computerized research existed. It wasn't as advanced as it is now. We were stringing together Boolean searches when I was in law school. And don't even get me started on Shepardizing cases." She shuddered.

"Boo-hoo what with a shepherd now?"

Sasha laughed. "Exactly. But relying on computerized legal research simply wasn't the Prescott way. Lawyers who started practicing when secretaries still took shorthand and pounded out briefs on manual typewriters didn't exactly trust the notion of feeding a string of words into a database and having it spit out an answer."

The digital native managed a hesitant nod and started to back away. "*Riiiiight.* Did you guys use leeches and stuff when you got sick, too?"

"Get out of here, already," Sasha shooed her. "You're distracting me. Leeches."

As Jordana slipped out into the hall and closed the door behind her with a soft click, she returned her attention to her caselaw.

The causes of action against Asher Morgan and Sentinel Solution Systems should've been clear cut. Of course, they weren't.

Morgan had made public information that his employer had promised to keep private. But it would be a stretch to characterize a list of names and zip codes as trade secret or proprietary information. And the man hadn't violated a nondisclosure or noncompetition agreement because he hadn't signed one.

Not to mention, a government contractor specializing in the interception, collection, and analysis of digital intelligence was in no way, shape, or form even remotely a competitor to a charitable crowdfunding community. Sentinel Solution Systems and DoGive-Thrive were as unrelated as two entities could be.

She sipped her coffee and moved on to the statutory provisions she'd printed. Pennsylvania's Breach of Personal Information Notification Act sounded promising. Although the purpose of the statute was to require the company in question to notify its customers of the breach, she hoped there'd be a hook she could use to snare Morgan and his new employer, as well.

She traded her pen for a highlighter and turned to the definition section. Morgan's action met the definition of a 'breach.' Good. The definition of a 'business' included nonprofit corporation. Even better. Maybe she'd found her angle.

She read on, but her optimism was short-lived. The act defined 'personal information' as a person's first initial or name and their last name in combination with or linked to a slew of possible information, including such items as unredacted social security numbers or credit card information. In fact, the act specifically excluded addresses and telephone numbers from the definition of personal information.

She tossed the now-useless statute to the side of her desk and turned to the federal law. The Computer Fraud and Abuse Act's focus was on criminal penalties, but it also provided for civil liability against a former employee and/or his new employer for damages arising from the unauthorized use of information from the former employer's computer system. Although the CFAA had been used civilly mainly to address the theft of computer information to gain a competitive advantage, she saw enough wiggle room in the definitions of 'damage' and 'loss' to hang her hat on. A federal statute would hold more sway over Sentinel Solution Systems, anyway.

She nodded to herself. She'd sue both defendants under the CFAA and add a claim against Asher Morgan for breach of his duty of loyalty, good faith and fair dealing during his employment. It wouldn't be difficult to establish that he'd intentionally engaged in acts contrary to DoGiveThrive's interests.

She pulled up a blank complaint template on her laptop and started typing. Her fingers flew over the keys. When she looked up, the sun was low in the sky and her coffee mug was empty. She spell-checked the draft, saved the document, and emailed it to Gella. Then she stood, stretched, and packed up her bag. Just before she turned out her office light, she scrolled through her cell phone notifications. No word from Connelly. But Hank had texted a picture of the twins and some of his kids putting on a puppet show.

She smiled down at the image and tried to ignore the growing pressure in her chest when she thought about Connelly.

This is stupid.

She pressed Connelly's name in her contact list and stood, with one hand on the light switch, waiting for the call to connect. It rolled straight to voicemail. She ended the call without leaving a message, clicked off the light, and stepped out into the hall.

Her phone rang in her hand.

"Leo?"

"Sorry? Sasha, it's me, Gella."

She took a breath. "No, I'm sorry. I just called my

husband and I thought you were him returning my call. You can't have reviewed the complaint already, have you?"

"What? No. I have terrible news. Essiah Wheaton is dead."

22

Leo rang Hank's doorbell then yawned, a wide open-mouthed yawn he made no effort to cover. He was bone-tired. The flight from Houston had been delayed and then delayed again. By the time he landed in Pittsburgh and retrieved his car, the early edge of rush hour was underway. So he'd inched his way along the clogged roads until he finally reached Hank's place.

He'd turned off his phone so that if Sasha tried to reach him, the call would go straight to voicemail. The coward's way, maybe. But he preferred to think of it as the survivor's way. The better course was to fight his way through snarled traffic, pick up the twins, grab takeout from her favorite Thai restaurant, and face the music in person.

Hank's middle boy opened the door.

"Hi," Mark said, before shouting over his shoulder into the interior of the house, "Dad, it's not Mrs. Connelly. It's *Mr.* Connelly."

Hank appeared in the hallway, and his mouth fell open when he spotted Leo. He smoothed his expression in a heartbeat.

"Thanks, pal. Why don't you help Finn and Fiona gather up their toys and pack their bag for me."

He waited for the boy to walk away. Then he said, "You got here fast."

Leo glanced down at his watch. "Not really."

"Sure you did. I only got word about an hour ago that Wheaton had been neutralized."

"Wait—what?"

"Someone working on Storm Chaser must be monitoring emergency and law enforcement communications. Ingrid called to say well done when the status on your assignment was updated to show that a coroner was dispatched to Essiah Wheaton's home. He was dead at that scene."

"Wheaton's dead?" Leo repeated. The words sounded dull and far away to his own ears.

Hank frowned. "Well, yeah. That was the idea. Remember?"

Leo spoke slowly. "I didn't kill him."

Hank stepped out onto his porch and pulled the door shut behind him. He stared hard at Leo.

"What do you mean you didn't kill him?"

"I mean I came straight here from the airport."

"Your assignment was to take care of Wheaton."

He locked eyes with his friend and boss. "I know. I came here to tell you to find somebody else to do it. But I guess you don't need to now."

They stared at one another for a long, tense moment.

Hank broke eye contact first when he passed his wide palm over his forehead. "I don't understand."

"Neither do I."

"If you didn't kill him, who did?"

"Probably whoever was crashing around in the woods last night. The question isn't who, though. It's why."

"This is bad," Hank muttered, more to himself than to Leo.

"So what now?"

"I have to ask—you really didn't kill him?"

"No. Look, my flight was delayed. I spent the time on the tarmac fighting for elbow room and wrestling with my conscience. Essiah Wheaton may have been a no-good piece of trash. But I'm a federal agent, not his executioner, judge, and jury. That's not how the system works—or, at least, that's not how it should work. I tried to imagine sitting down for dinner across from Sasha or tucking Finn and Fiona in for the night with Essiah Wheaton's blood on my hands and I couldn't. So I came here to tell you that." He exhaled.

He'd rehearsed his speech in his head during the interminable drive from the airport. It struck a weirdly hollow note now that the man he was refusing to kill was dead.

Hank shook his head. "Let's keep this between us for now. As far as Ingrid and the boys at the NCTC are concerned, you completed your mission. But this could get real messy, real fast. You need to get up to Wheaton's place and figure out what the hell is going on."

He was right. His mea culpa to Sasha would have to wait. "You can keep the kids until Sasha finishes up at work?"

"Yes. She texted me that she's on her way, though, so get out of here."

Just then, the door opened. Mark had Leo's hiking backpack in one hand and was being trailed by Finn and Fiona.

"Daddy!"

Oh, crap.

He crouched and swept them into a bear hug, one on each side of him. Then he planted a kiss on each of their faces.

"Hey, monkeys. I just stopped by real quick to say hi. Did you have fun with Uncle Hank and the kids today?"

"Oh, yes."

"We played all day. No naps!"

They answered right over one another.

He managed a smile. "Great. I have to do a favor for Uncle Hank. Mommy's on her way to get you. I'll see you tonight, okay?"

"Okay," they chorused.

Hank coughed. "Maybe don't tell your mom that Dad stopped by," he suggested. "It can be your secret."

"Right. Don't tell Mommy you saw me. That way we can surprise her later," Leo said.

"Oh, a secret," Fiona said, clearly pleased by the idea.

"And a surprise!" Finn added.

"Great. Go on back inside until Mommy gets here." Leo waved cheerfully until they disappeared back inside the house.

He straightened to standing.

"Go clean up your mess." Hank's voice was as grim as his face.

Leo nodded then turned and took the stairs down to

the sidewalk two at a time. He needed to get out of there before his wife showed up. If he was quick about it, he could stop by the house to change his clothes and pick up some essentials and be out of there before she showed up with the twins.

23

Fletcher squeezed the phone between his ear and his neck and cracked his knuckles while he waited for Chuck to pick up. As he listened to the incessant ringing, he started with his left index finger, pulling on the digit until the knuckle joint gave a satisfying pop and then moving on to the next. He reached the middle finger of his right hand before Chuck finally answered the blasted phone.

"Sorry." His head of security spoke in a low voice, just above a whisper.

"What's going on? Did you handle our problem?"

"I did. It just took a little longer than we'd anticipated."

Chuck sounded nervous. Fletcher didn't like that, not one bit.

"How come?"

"Well, he was in for the night last night, obviously, so we found a motel just outside town. We figured we'd hit the hay and get up early today, set up on the road between his place and town and take a shot at him when he rode by on his motorcycle."

Fletcher nodded to himself. It was a decent plan. Wheaton would be exposed, a soft target. And he'd likely lose control of his bike and crash. Hell, if they got lucky his fuel tank would explode, making the cleanup and forensics work problematic.

"But? He didn't go in to town?"

"Oh, no. He did. But his wife or whoever she is was on the back of the bike. And you said—"

"I know what I said. I didn't mean you should get all dainty about it. For Chrissake, Chuck, sometimes there's collateral damage."

"Yes, sir. But Marcus was insistent we not hurt her."

He heard a trace of blame in Chuck's voice. As if this were his fault for saddling Chuck with a greenhorn.

In fairness, it probably was. The rank and file of the Brotherhood were dependable men who embraced the ideals and stood firm for their heritage. But they weren't stone-cold killers, no matter how the liberal media liked to paint them. No, his warrior soldiers, while fierce and merciless, were few. And Marcus sure as shooting wasn't one of them.

But, he'd be damned if he'd concede the point to Chuck now, in the middle of an operation.

He waited in steely silence until Chuck went on.

After a pause, Chuck continued, "They were gone all dang day, so after lunch we went back to the house and took a closer look at the place."

"How close of a look?"

"We let ourselves in."

"For crying out loud—"

"Don't worry. I talked Marcus through how to pick the lock. We wore gloves, and I didn't touch anything. Nobody's going to find my prints at the scene. And he's not in the system."

He unclenched his jaw. "Did you find anything?"

"No. Marcus did a search, real precise. He didn't toss the place or anything. He did a good job, Fletch. The wife won't find a thing out of place. While he looked for anything that might tie Wheaton to us, I kept a lookout. They have this big picture window, it takes up the whole front wall of their den. I watched the road through my binoculars. Right around three o'clock, I saw them coming back."

"Tell me you got out of there."

"Relax, already. We got out in plenty of time. We couldn't go back to the car the way we came; we'd have had to walk right past them. So we looped around behind the garage out back. Wheaton pulled up to the house and let his gal off at the door then drove the motorcycle up to the garage. It's more of a barn, really. So, he killed the engine and put down the kickstand. He had to pull the door up manually. That's when I realized the barn was the best place to do it."

"You killed him in his garage? Are you crazy? She had to hear the shot."

"She might've. If I'd shot him. But I strangled him."

"You strangled Essiah."

"Right. I was still wearing the gloves. I slipped into the garage behind him while he was wheeling his bike inside. Then I killed him."

"Did he get a look at your face?"

"I don't know. It doesn't matter. He's deader than a coyote plastered across the highway." Chuck's voice was like whiskey, smooth and velvety.

He had a point. "Then what?"

"Then I dragged him out of the view of the doorway and shoved him under his workbench."

"Why?"

"So she wouldn't see his body from the kitchen

window. The way I figured it, she'd glance out back, see the garage door raised and assume he was out there tinkering with his bike or something. It might take her a while to come looking for him. Makes time of death trickier if she doesn't find him until dinner's ready or what have you."

"Smart."

"Yeah. And good thing I pulled him over to the workbench."

"Why's that?"

"Because Marcus came in to help me. Dead weight's heavy, man."

"Hence the name."

"What?"

"Never mind. So Marcus came in."

"And after we crammed Wheaton under the bench, Marcus cracked his noggin on the underside of the worktable."

"Why am I not surprised?"

"It's a good thing he did. That snake Wheaton had taped an envelope under there. A big orange envelope that said 'OPEN IN CASE OF MY DEATH' across the front."

"That dirty bastard." Fletch's heart was hammering. If Marcus hadn't hit his head ... he couldn't even think about it. He caught his breath. But Marcus *had* hit his head. They had the envelope. They were safe.

"He's dirtier than you think. It's not in there."

"Come again?"

"The proof he took. It's not in there, Fletch. We opened it up and all that was in there was some sappy note to his girl, who isn't Karen, by the way. Though she sure does favor her. But the note's addressed to 'My Darling Shelia Anne.' Anyhow, here, let me read it to you:

My Darling Sheila Anne,

If you're reading this, I've been killed by some very bad men.

But don't worry. They won't hurt you. If anything happens to you, I've made arrangements for information about them to go public. It's a little post-life insurance policy.

I loved you every day and I'm missing you already. I'll be waiting for you at the Gates of Heaven.

Yours eternally,

Essiah

And that's all that was in the envelope."

Fletch pounded his fist into the wall. He always thought 'my blood was boiling' was just an expression, but now he wasn't so sure. He felt some internal fire spreading through his body, threatening to combust. That wily SOB had outsmarted him. He'd hidden evidence that could send Fletch, Chuck, and a whole mess of others to prison for the rest of their lives. And now, he'd gone and killed the man without so much as a clue as to where it was and how to find it and destroy it.

Think.

He was trying, but it was hard, what with the way his heart was racing and his pulse was pounding in his ears.

"Uh, Fletcher?"

"I'm thinking."

"Right. I'm just wondering … I think Marcus and I need to make ourselves scarce, you know? Any reason we can't hightail it out of town?"

"I said, I'm thinking. Stop your yammering for a minute."

Chuck fell silent.

Fletch thought. Essiah Wheaton was nobody's fool. If there was one envelope, there could be more, scattered around his property so his widow would be sure to find at least one. Nothing he could do about that.

And if he was telling the truth, somewhere, someone was sitting on information they planned to share with … the public? What did that mean? The authorities? The media? Could be anybody. Nothing much he could do about that without knowing who was supposed to pull the trigger on the release.

But surely the plan would only go into motion if this mystery person believed 'very bad men' had killed Wheaton. Fletch smiled. Now *that* he could do something about. And it would kill two birds with one stone.

"You got some pictures of that fed last night, right?"

"Yeah, why?"

"Go to an office supply store—not in town, someplace else—and print a handful of shots of him creeping around the property. Try and get it so the time and date stamp shows on the bottom. Take out that blasted note and stuff the pictures in that envelope of Wheaton's."

"How come?"

"His darlin' Sheila Anne may know to look for an envelope somewhere if he dies. We're gonna make sure she finds one and that it points to this federal agent as the killer."

Fletcher heard the comprehension take hold as Chuck let out a low whistle. "That's brilliant. She'll think the feds killed her man, and this guy holding the dirt won't release it because he's only supposed to if *we* kill Wheaton."

"That's the general idea."

"It could work."

"It better."

"Should we tape it back under the worktable, where we found it?"

"No. That's gonna be an active crime scene. We want the woman to find it. Not the cops. Put it—I dunno—in the back of her freezer. She's probably gonna be in and out the next couple days making funeral arrangements or what have you. You'll have plenty of chances."

He heard Marcus's voice, urgent and fast, on the other end.

"What's Marcus blabbering about?"

"He asked if I can handle this without him. He wants to go home."

"Boo-freakin-hoo. No, he stays with you. And, Chuck?"

"Yeah?"

"If he becomes a problem ..."

"I know."

That was one of the things Fletcher liked about Chuck. He *did* know without having to be told every blasted thing.

"Good. And once that's done, you two are gonna have to hole up there for at least a little while. If we can flush out Wheaton's ally, that's even better. We don't need that threat hanging over our heads for all eternity. Even if this misdirection works, it's a loose end."

"I hear you. Wheaton didn't work at the bank in

town, but maybe he had a safe deposit box there or something. I'll poke around after we take care of the envelope."

"Good man. For the Brotherhood."

"For the Brotherhood," Chuck echoed.

24

Sasha only half-listened to Hank's report of Finn and Fiona's day. She smiled absently, shouldered the backpack, and thanked him for his help. The entire time, her brain was replaying her conversation with Gella.

Gella had tried again to reach Essiah Wheaton. A woman answered the phone. Gella said it was clear that she'd been crying. When Gella apologized for disturbing her, the woman broke down and explained her husband had been murdered in their backyard earlier in the evening. Gella had called on her seminary training to comfort the newly widowed Mrs. Wheaton. Something Gella'd said must've struck a chord with the woman, because she asked Gella to come see her. And,

Gella, being Gella, had promised to drive out to Mars in the morning.

Sasha was of two minds about this plan. Her lawyer brain thought it was a foolish, possibly dangerous, idea. Her human being brain thought it was a kind, compassionate gesture. In the end, humanity won. But she insisted that Gella let her tag along, just in case damage control proved necessary.

Gella refused to consider the idea that Wheaton's death could be related in any way to the data leak. She insisted it was just a coincidence.

Sasha hoped her client was right, but she'd seen too many so-called coincidences caused by killers to dismiss the possibility. She wished Connelly would turn up so she could bounce her wild theories off him. He was her most trusted sounding board. But he was gone.

As if her daughter could read her thoughts, Fiona piped up, "Daddy will be home soon."

Her lilting voice broke through and caught Sasha's full attention.

"I hope so, honey."

Her daughter looked up at her. "It's a secret."

"And a surprise!" Finn chimed in.

She turned to Finn. "Did Uncle Hank tell you that?"

He pressed his lips shut and looked at his sister for guidance.

Fiona wagged a finger at him. "Daddy said don't tell."

"Daddy was at Hank's house?" Sasha probed. Her voice crackled with urgency and searched her children's faces to see which of them would cave first.

They wore identical looks. Their foreheads scrunched up with worry, their eyes wide and uncertain.

She took a breath and pasted on a wide, reassuring smile. "Never mind. If it's a secret surprise, you shouldn't tell me."

They resumed walking. Finn's shoulders relaxed. Fiona skipped in time to some vaguely familiar tune she hummed.

Having stopped herself from deposing her three-year olds until they cracked and dooming them to a life of therapy, she turned her frustration inward. Her husband was up to something, he was keeping her in the dark, and she just knew he was in trouble.

A heavy helplessness settled over her chest. The realization that the tables were turned—that she put him in this exact spot on a regular basis—made the weight even heavier.

Lost in thought, she forgot all about her plan to stop at the grocery store. She was unlocking the door when she realized she had nothing to feed the kids for dinner. She ushered them inside, rested the back of her head against the wall just inside the door, kicked off her high heels, closed her eyes, and managed a wry laugh. Maybe Connelly was right—this place was falling apart without him, and he hadn't even been gone a full twenty-four hours.

Mocha ran toward her from the kitchen and nudged her hand with a wet nose. She opened her eyes. "And I guess you want to go outside, huh?"

She ruffled the dog's fur and led him to the kitchen then put him out back in the yard. A walk would have to wait. She filled Java's food and water bowls under the cat's watchful eye.

Then she rummaged through the refrigerator. No dinner ingredients had magically appeared while she'd been working. But Connelly did have a couple craft beers nestled on the bottom shelf. She grabbed one and dug through the utensil drawer for a bottle opener. She pried off the cap and took a long swallow of the cold, heavy stout.

Finn and Fiona had made a beeline for their craft table. They sat across from each other sharing a package of fat crayons. She walked over and watched them work for a moment. Finn used slow, careful crayon strokes to create a series of concentric circles that were more or less circular. Fiona, the tip of her tongue poking out of her mouth as she concentrated, scribbled wildly, her lines arcing off the paper and onto the laminated tabletop.

"Hey, artists. Mommy's going to change her clothes and then we'll have breakfast for dinner! Isn't that funny? Eggs, and toast, and a big fruit salad."

They bobbed their heads in agreement but never looked up from their masterpieces.

She let the dog back in then hurried upstairs to change while the twins were still occupied. After she pulled on a pair of sweatpants and an old tee-shirt, she called her parents' number to ask them to watch the kids tomorrow.

She squeezed the phone between her ear and shoulder so she could toss a load of laundry into the washer while she begged for the favor.

"Of course, Sunshine," her mother cooed in response to her request. Her voice was somehow just slightly *too* soothing. "We'd love to spend the day with Finn and Fiona."

She opened the door to the washing machine and frowned. The clothes Connelly had been wearing last night were already in the drum. She lifted his shirt out and stared at it.

He'd been here? And hadn't stuck around to see them? Or even left a note?

Her mom's voice broke through the thoughts racing

around in her mind. "Honey, did you hear me? What time do you need us?"

"Sorry. I'll drop them off at seven."

"Don't be silly, Dad will come get them. It'll be easier for you."

"Okay. Great." She tried to rush her mother off the phone.

But Valentina was impervious to her efforts. "Where did you say Leo is? You sound stressed. Is everything okay?"

"Everything's fine. I just ... it's a case. I can't really talk about it. You know, it's privileged."

"Of course. What bad timing, a difficult case while Leo's out of town for work."

The note of concern in her mother's voice made tears prick at her eyes. She dropped the shirt back into the washing machine and pressed her palms against her eyelids, willing the tears not to well up.

"He'll be home tomorrow night, for sure?"

"For sure," she lied.

She said goodbye to her mother then sat on the edge of her bed and drained the bottle of beer.

What if Connelly doesn't come home tomorrow?

The carefully constructed don't ask-don't tell policy that formed the foundation of their life seemed to be crumbling around her.

Leo navigated the highways back to Mars on autopilot, relying on his anterior cingulate cortex to keep him on the road while he focused on Wheaton's death. As the SUV rolled north on Interstate 79, he ticked through the common motives for murder: passion, in the guise of love, hate, or jealousy; money or greed; a dispute or vendetta; revenge; and protecting a secret. Assuming the man hadn't been assassinated by a government agent, one of these was likely the reason he was dead.

And the best way to narrow the options was through humint—human intelligence. A clinical, bureaucratic label for what amounted to gossip. He imagined the small borough's rumor mill would be working overtime in response to a shocking murder.

For a variety of reasons, his first stop was the large, bright all-night diner on the outskirts of town. First, he was sure tongues would be wagging inside. Second, he hadn't eaten since he'd grabbed a chicken sandwich at the Houston airport nine hours earlier. Low blood sugar and investigative work were a poor match.

He took a seat at the counter and paged through the laminated menu.

"What'll be?" the tall, auburn-haired waitress asked.

"I'll have a turkey and Swiss on rye and a side of fries."

"Anything to drink?"

"Just water for now, thanks."

She jotted down the order and disappeared into the kitchen. He surveyed the room. A handful of late diners focused more on their meals than chit chat. He didn't want to be the one to bring up the murder, so he waited.

It wasn't a long wait.

After a few minutes, the woman sitting three stools away caught his eye over her bowl of chicken noodle soup. Her brown eyes glittered from behind a pair of cat's eye glasses.

"Did ya' hear about Essiah Wheaton?"

He nodded. "Terrible."

She *tsk-tsked*, half-somber, half-titillated. "I heard his wife found the body."

The waitress dropped off Leo's water then leaned across the counter and said to the woman with the glasses in a loud whisper, "Well, *I* heard the FBI took control of the crime scene."

Leo lowered his eyes to the counter and listened intently.

"Wonder why? Do you think he could've been mixed up in drugs?"

"No, that's the DEA, not the FBI," the waitress said with authority.

He sipped his water. Of course, the Bureau would try to wrest the investigation from the local authorities—they thought Wheaton had been targeted by the task force. He wondered what they'd do once they realized it hadn't been a government kill.

"Well, whatever happened out there at their place, it's a crying shame."

"Amen."

The gossipy woman shook her head sadly, paid her bill, and slipped off the stool. "Bye, Dana," she called to the waitress as she left.

"Turkey up!" A voice shouted from the kitchen.

Dana grabbed the plate from the pass separating the kitchen from the dining room and plunked it down in front of Leo along with a bottle of ketchup.

"Enjoy your dinner."

"Thanks. So, this Wheaton guy who died—they think he was murdered?"

She gave him a look. For a moment, he thought she was going to tell him to mind his own business, but the undercurrent of excitement must have won out over her sense of propriety.

As she walked away to take care of a couple sitting at one of the booths, she said, "They're sure he was murdered. Stan, the cook, has an uncle who's a medic. He says Essiah was strangled."

Leo nearly choked on his french fry. Strangled, not shot from a distance. He didn't pretend to know the standard operating procedure of *every* shadow agency in the U.S. Government. But he did know plenty. And, to his knowledge, there wasn't a team whose SOP was to strangle targets. Which meant Wheaton's killer almost certainly hadn't acted at the direction of the Project Storm Chaser Task Force.

Which meant, what?

While he chewed his sandwich, he turned the new piece of information over in his mind as if it were an odd-shaped piece he was trying to fit into a jigsaw puzzle. He finished his meal without an answer.

"Did you leave room for dessert?" Dana asked.

"Always." He ordered a slice of the cranberry-apple pie and a cup of coffee.

While he waited, he thumbed through his phone, scanning his messages. He started to type a message to Sasha, thought better of it, and deleted the text unsent. He turned off notifications and shoved the phone back into his pocket.

"Here you go." She placed a generous wedge of pie, a mug of coffee, and a handful of creamers on the counter in front of him.

"It looks great. Thanks. Did Wheaton have a family?" He picked up the fork and attacked the pie as if it were more interesting than the answer to his question.

She narrowed her eyes and studied him from under her thick eyelashes, made even thicker by a heavy coat of mascara. He could tell she was weighing whether she should answer, so he glanced up and flashed her a smile.

"I have twins—they're three. A tragedy like that ... it just makes a guy think, you know?"

The suspicion drained from her expression and her eyes softened. "Three-year-old twins, huh? Bet they keep you busy."

He laughed. "You know it."

She shook her head and her curly ponytail swung over her shoulder. "Mr. and Mrs. Wheaton didn't have kids. I suppose that's a blessing."

"But he was married?"

"Yeah. Newlyweds, I think. She actually doesn't go by Wheaton—she's one of those gals who kept her maiden name. Funny, because she never struck me as the type."

"You're friendly with her then?"

Another quick, lidded look. He was pushing it, he knew. He prepared to back off, but she answered.

"I wouldn't say we're best friends or anything. I

mean, they only moved here about eight or nine months ago. But, sure, I know her. We don't get a lot of transplants around here, you know? Sheila Anne and Essiah were both from Texas."

"Is that right?"

"Yeah. And my boyfriend and Essiah rode together sometimes—"

"Motorcycles."

"That's right. How'd you know?"

"We have—or had—a mutual friend, Essiah and I."

"Oh? Do you know C.J., then? That's my boyfriend."

"I've met him. He's one heckuva Scrabble player."

She laughed. "Not really. Essiah and their pal Slim were the real Scrabble players. C.J.'s more of a chess player. I never could get the hang of it."

The couple seated in a booth on the other side of the diner were staring at them. When Leo caught the man's eye, he gestured to their mugs.

"I think one of your other tables is looking for refills," he said, pointing to the pair.

She grabbed a white carafe from the counter and hurried in their direction.

He sipped his coffee and reviewed what he'd just learned. He could rule out two possibilities fairly easily.

As newlyweds, the odds were good that Wheaton and his wife were in love. Although a jealous ex or a stalker couldn't be ruled out, it seemed unlikely that one of them had been carrying on an extramarital affair. And women rarely strangled men. It was a matter of strength and size. So, the murder was probably not a crime of passion.

As newcomers to the town—and outsiders—the couple likely hadn't had time to make any local enemies. The sorts of disputes and vendettas that pitted neighbor against neighbor hardened over years, generations even. Property line squabbles, kids dating and breaking up, or even something as mundane as umpiring a little league game could get a guy killed. But not in the space of months.

That left money, revenge, and a secret as contenders that merited a closer look. He considered each in turn.

Money was a possibility, but it seemed like a stretch. Wheaton and Sheila Anne Whatever-Her-Name-Was didn't live extravagantly. No flashy cars or in-ground pool. The house was well-maintained but modest. Leo'd seen nothing that would suggest the man owed the wrong guy money or was otherwise having financial problems. It was possible he was the secret heir to a fortune and someone had killed him to keep him from inheriting. Besides, this was real life, not a soap opera, and, on a basic gut-check level, Wheaton's death didn't seem to be related to finances.

Leo could, however, easily see Wheaton's killer strangling the man to keep a secret or as an act of revenge for some past wrong. Or both, actually. If Wheaton *had* been involved with the Heritage Brotherhood and he'd crossed them, revenge was a strong possibility. And even if he just knew where the proverbial—or, with these guys, actual—bodies were buried, they'd have plenty of incentive to make sure he never talked.

The waitress returned with his check and placed it face down on the table. "I'm sorry about your friend."

"I'm sorry, too. I didn't know him that well, but it's a helluva a way to go."

She set her mouth in a grim line. "Slim says the guys at Mugsy's are getting all worked up about it. Essiah was one of theirs, even though he hadn't been here very long. People don't just get themselves *strangled* around here, you know?"

He nodded his agreement.

Mugsy's was on his list of establishments to visit. But now that he had some food in his stomach, he needed to find a hotel room.

Once he'd had a ninety-minute nap and a hot shower, he'd be ready to walk into a bar full of Essiah's mourning, possibly half-drunk, biker buddies.

25

The twins were sleeping. The dog was sleeping. The cat was sleeping.

Sasha glanced at the clock hanging on the wall over Connelly's desk. It was just past two o'clock in the morning. The whole world was sleeping.

Her phone buzzed to announce the arrival of an email. *Leo?* Her heart jumped and she lunged for the device.

She scanned the envelope information.

Not Leo.

Apparently Gella couldn't sleep either. Sasha opened the attachment to the message and began to review Gella's comments to the complaint.

At two thirty, she padded downstairs to make a pot of coffee. She leaned against the counter and thumbed out a text to Connelly while the coffee brewed. She stared down at the screen willing a response to appear. One did not.

She filled her mug and trudged back upstairs.

By five o'clock, she'd revised the complaint; had sent it back to her insomniac client and gotten approval to file it; and had uploaded it to the Western District of Pennsylvania electronic court filing system.

Her head was buzzing from exhaustion and her vision was beginning to blur. She typed a quick message to Gella, copying Naya, to let them know the complaint had been filed. Then she checked her phone for what had to be the hundredth time. Still no word from her husband.

She drained the last of the reheated coffee from her mug, headed to the kitchen to put on a fresh pot, and tiptoed back up the stairs to take a shower. She might as well start her day.

She stood under the hot spray of water for a long time, trying to wash away the film of worry and uncertainty about what was going on with Connelly.

After she dried off, she wrapped her hair in a thick towel and cinched her robe around her waist to go to the kitchen and get yet another mug of coffee.

When she returned to the bathroom to blow-dry her hair, her phone's notification light was blinking. She put the mug down in a hurry. Hot coffee splashed over the side and scalded the back of her hand. She wiped off the coffee on a towel and grabbed the phone from the vanity.

One missed call. No messages.

She swiped across the telephone app to open it. Connelly had called three minutes ago.

Her hands shook as she hit the call back button.

Please pick up. Please pick up. Please pick up.

The call rolled straight to voicemail. She listened to Connelly's familiar voice as he instructed her to leave a message. She racked her brain for a suitable message but came up with nothing.

She disconnected the call and buried her face in her hands so her crying wouldn't wake the twins.

Leo felt like warmed-over crap. Partly, because he'd left his wife in a lurch with no explanation. Partly, because he'd spent the hours from approximately midnight until after five a.m. nursing first bottles of beer and then glasses of whiskey with Wheaton's buddies.

He hadn't learned anything of value, but he'd managed to embed himself into the circle of the man's friends. When Bill the bartender had announced that it was closing time and flipped on the bright overhead lights to chase out the stragglers, Leo hadn't been asked to leave. Slim, C.J., and some of the others headed into the back and made themselves comfortable in what had once been a break room for the catering staff. He'd tagged along.

After Bill had cleaned up the bar and locked up for the night, he'd joined them with a bottle of single-barrel bourbon, which they'd worked their way through, telling stories about Wheaton. Leo kept his contributions vague and leaned heavily on the hour or so he'd spent in Hyacinth for material.

Once people started draping themselves across benches and snoring, he asked Bill to unlock the door so he could leave. He figured even the worst hotel mattress would be a step up from a metal bench.

Bill confirmed that he was okay to drive, told him he was welcome to come back for a brunch in Essiah's honor at ten-thirty, then locked the door behind him.

Leo squinted into the brightening sky for a moment and yawned open-mouthed. Then, as he trudged to his SUV, he pulled out his phone, filled with a sudden need to hear Sasha's voice.

After four rings, the call went to voicemail. He disconnected and frowned down at his phone. Sasha usually started her day before the sun. He'd thought he'd catch her while the twins were still sleeping, but she hadn't picked up.

You should be glad she didn't answer. What are you planning to tell her? Hi, honey, I'm in the wind because someone else killed the man I was supposed to kill and now I have to find out who did it. Yeah, that would go over great.

No, he had to fix this mess in Mars first. Then he could turn his full attention to making things right with Sasha. It was smart, logical. The right decision. Even if it felt like a huge, possibly irreparable, mistake.

He pocketed the phone, turned the key in the ignition, and stared bleary-eyed out at the road.

26

Sasha was grateful she was in a hurry when her dad showed up. On the list of topics she wanted to discuss with her father, her missing husband didn't make the cut.

"Hi, Dad. The kids have had breakfast. Pets have been fed. It would be awesome if you guys could take Mocha for a walk. Lunch is in the fridge. I've got an early meeting in Mars, but I won't be late tonight. Bye!" She downloaded the information to him in one breath as she slipped on her shoes and grabbed her keys, jacket, and bag.

On her way out the door, she paused to admire the block castle Finn and Fiona were constructing. She kissed the top of each of their heads.

"Bye-bye, Mommy," Finn said.

"Daddy's coming home?" Fiona wanted to know.

"Mmm-hmm," Sasha managed to choke out around the lump in her throat.

"Yay!"

She rushed out the door before she lost her tenuous grip on her emotions.

She fed Essiah Wheaton's address into her station wagon's navigation system and activated the hands-free calling function through her speakers.

"Call Naya."

Calling Naya, her car told her. Or maybe it was her phone. Whichever. Some inanimate object was talking to her.

"Hey, Mac."

"Hi. Listen, do me a favor and let Caroline and Will know I'll be in later this morning."

"Yeah, I saw the time on the docket system. You filed that complaint in the middle of the night. Gonna send Leo and the kids to the park and catch up on your beauty sleep?"

"I wish. He's ... out of town. My parents are taking the kids, but I'm on my way out to Mars for a meeting."

"There's nothing on your calendar," Naya mused.

"Right. That's why I'm calling. Gella set up a meeting, and I don't think she should attend it without counsel."

"Really? Do I need to be there?"

Sasha knew Naya wasn't being territorial. After all, she was the relationship partner with this client. But she also suspected Naya wouldn't want to touch this matter with someone else's ten-foot pole.

"I don't think so."

"It's about the litigation—already? You only just filed."

"It's related to the data leak." She removed one hand from the steering wheel and picked up her travel mug. She sipped her ice water and wished it were coffee. Her doctor had warned her she'd end up with a peptic ulcer if she didn't exhibit some modicum of restraint. So, she'd reformed: she now drank a full glass of water between her first and second pots of coffee each day.

"Spit it out."

For half a second, she thought Naya had read her mind about the water. "Oh, right. You know how Gella wasn't able to get in touch with that man who donated all the money to the hurricane relief projects? The one whose name was on the government's list?"

"Sure, Mr. Wheaton. Are you two going to see him personally?"

"Not exactly."

"Mac ...." Naya's voice held a warning note. Her patience was thinning.

"We're going to see his widow. Apparently, Mr. Wheaton was murdered yesterday evening."

"Oh, sweet Lord. You think it's related?"

"Do I? I think it might be. Gella doesn't. But she's a trusting soul."

"Listen, be careful up there. If the NCTC is behind this—"

"I know."

"It's too bad Leo's out of town. Maybe take Hank with you? You know, for backup."

She'd considered the idea, but at this point, her anger toward her husband was bleeding over toward his boss. She didn't want to ask Hank for any more favors.

"We'll be fine."

"I don't know. This seems like a bad idea."

"Gella's driving out there whether I do or not. Which seems like a worse idea—to go and make sure she doesn't say anything stupid or let her fly solo?"

Naya blew out a loud breath. "You're right, I guess."

"Believe me, I don't like this any more than you do."

She glanced at her navigation screen and was about to end the call when Naya said, "Hang on a second."

Two short beeps let her know she'd been placed on hold. She raised her eyebrows and drank some more water. Then she reached across to the passenger seat and rummaged blindly through her bag with her right hand until she found a slightly crushed protein bar.

She was tearing the wrapper open with her teeth when Naya came back on the line.

"Sorry about that. Caroline just took an urgent message for you. She wanted me to pass it on."

She dropped the bar in her lap. "Urgent? Did something happen to Leo? Oh, no not one of the kids?"

Naya didn't comment on her rare use of her husband's first name. "Leo? No. Wait—where *is* he?"

"I don't know."

The statement hung between them for a silent moment.

"Oh. But, no, it's not Leo. And it's not your kids. Your family's fine. It's urgent in the trial attorney sense of the word. But it is odd."

"Oh." She exhaled and loosened her grip on the steering wheel. "What is it?"

"Apparently Asher Morgan and Sentinel Solution Systems have already retained counsel. Someone named Angela Washington called. She told Caroline she's representing both defendants."

"Washington? Never heard of her. But that's not that unusual—why wouldn't they enter into a joint defense agreement?"

"No, that's not the weird part. She told Caroline she has a time-sensitive settlement offer to convey to you. Her clients are willing to, and this is a quote, "make it worth DoGiveThrive's while" to settle the case."

She blinked. "That's fast."

"No kidding. There's more. Attorney Washington said she's authorized to offer a mid-six figure amount. But the offer expires at noon."

Naya's words filled the passenger compartment of the car.

Sasha tried to figure out what they could mean.

"Are you still there?" Naya asked.

"I'm here. But that's ... that doesn't make a lick of sense."

"I know. What do you think they're up to?"

Her stomach tightened. "I don't have the faintest idea, but I know this much. It's nothing good. Will you text me Angela Washington's telephone number? I'm going to see if I can get a hold of Gella and have her meet me somewhere to talk this over before we go to see Wheaton's widow."

"I'll send it as soon as I hang up," she promised. "And remember, be—"

"I'm always careful, Naya."

"Could've fooled me." Naya got in the last word with

the retort and hurriedly ended the call before Sasha could respond.

Sasha jabbed the button to silence her directions and instructed her phone to call Gella Pinkney. The tinny ringing of the phone came through the speakers.

"Sasha?" Gella answered on the fourth ring, slightly out of breath. "You're not already there, are you?"

"No, I'm about fifteen minutes away. What about you?"

"Um, it looks like I must be about three or four minutes behind you. I'm sorry we couldn't drive up together, but I need to head straight to Ohio after we talk to Ms. Johnson."

"Johnson?"

"Essiah Wheaton's widow. She kept her maiden name."

"Oh, right, of course. No worries about driving separately. But we should talk before we meet with Ms. Johnson." She spotted a diner just off the exit she was approaching. "Why don't I buy you a quick breakfast?—there's a diner just ahead on the right."

"We shouldn't be late ..."

"I agree. But counsel for Mr. Morgan and his new employer called my office with a settlement offer that expires at noon. And I know you need to leave straight from our meeting with Ms. Johnson. So we need to talk beforehand."

"A settlement offer, already? That's awfully fast, isn't it?"

"I'd call it unprecedented speed."

"Sasha, what's going on?"

"I wish I knew. So about that breakfast?"

"Let's just make it a cup of coffee. I really don't want to keep Ms. Johnson waiting. She has funeral arrangements to make and a whole host of details to attend to."

"Of course. Coffee's great." She exited the highway and turned into the parking lot. "I'll grab a table and order the drinks to speed things along."

"See you in a few minutes."

Sasha pulled into a spot and retrieved her half-eaten energy bar from her lap. She finished eating the bar, drank the rest of her water, and headed into the restaurant to wait for Gella.

Gella walked through the door just after Sasha had ordered two coffees from a very cranky, tired-looking waitress whose nametag read Dana.

"No food?" she asked pointedly.

"We're in a hurry," Sasha explained as Gella slid into the booth across from her.

Dana huffed out a breath and rolled her eyes before walking away with the menus tucked under her arm.

"So what's this about a settlement offer?" Gella asked without preamble.

Sasha noted the bags pouching out from under Gella's eyes but didn't comment on her tired appearance. She knew she didn't exactly look well-rested herself. She'd made a weak attempt to conceal the dark half-moons under her own eyes with makeup. They looked like exactly what they were: two women who hadn't slept.

"I haven't called defense counsel back yet. I wanted to talk to you first. Her message said her clients are prepared to pay DoGiveThrive six figures to settle the claims in the complaint. But the offer is only good until noon."

Dana returned with two mugs of coffee and deposited them on the table. She reached into her apron pocket and removed a handful of creamers, which she tossed down beside the coffees.

"Thank you," Sasha said.

"Yes, thanks. Is your shift almost over?" Gella asked in a warm, interested voice.

The waitress pursed her lips. "My shift was over nearly an hour ago. But the morning guy didn't show up. So here I am."

"Ugh. I'm sorry," Sasha said.

"Not half as sorry as I am." She pushed her bangs

out of her eyes with the back of her hand. "Although, I guess I should cut him some slack. A friend of his died last night. He was up most of the drinking and reminiscing with his buddies."

The most recent population figures for Butler County showed fewer than two thousand residents living in Mars.

"Your co-worker knew Essiah Wheaton?" Sasha guessed.

Surprise sparked in the woman's tired eyes. "Yeah, he did. You ladies knew him, too?"

"In a manner of speaking," Gella explained. "We're actually on our way to see his widow."

"Ah, poor Sheila. Please tell her Dana's praying for her. I'll stop by tonight with a casserole."

"We will," Gella assured her. "I hope you get some rest."

"Thanks. Here's your bill, since you're in a hurry." She tore the top sheet of paper from her little pad and placed it face down on the table.

She started to walk away then turned back to Sasha. "I'm sorry I was short with you."

"No apology needed. You're just tired—trust me, I get it. I have three-year-old twins at home. I've been there." Sasha smiled at her.

She cocked her head. "That's funny. I waited on a guy last night who has three-year-old twins, too."

Sasha laughed politely and watched her walk away. Through a dull fog, her exhausted brain tried to grab hold of something the waitress had said. Something important, but the words slipped out of reach.

"Sasha? The settlement offer?" Gella prompted her gently as she peeled open a creamer cup and stirred the contents into her coffee.

Sasha shook her head to clear out the cobwebs, as her dad liked to say.

"Sorry, I got distracted." She took a drink of coffee and refocused. "It's highly unusual to get a substantial settlement offer this soon after filing suit. And it's unheard of to have such a short time to decide whether to accept it."

"It's almost as if Asher and Sentinel Solution Systems are trying to make this go away because they have something to hide," her client mused.

"No, it's exactly as if that's what they're doing."

"So, I should say no?"

Sasha rubbed a hand over her eyes. "It's a generous offer. And, as you and I talked about, proving that DoGiveThrive has been damaged and establishing a dollar amount will be tricky."

"So I should take it?"

She hemmed. “Let me put it another way. It’s a generous, but worrying, offer. It just *feels* wrong. Why don’t I call Ms. Washington while we’re on our way to Sheila Johnson’s house? I’ll try to tease out some more information and a get a sense of her clients’ motivation.”

“I suppose.”

“Besides, I imagine you’ll need to run the offer and your response past your Board?”

“Ordinarily, yes. But we won’t have time for that,” Gella fretted.

“Oh, I’ll push back against the noon deadline—hard. It’s ludicrous to extend a settlement offer with a four-hour shelf life. If nothing else, she ought to be willing to give you more time.”

Gella chewed on her lip, nodding. “And, I suppose if she’s not, that would tell us something.”

“It would.”

And if it turned out Washington wasn’t bluffing and the offer did expire at noon, it would be an expensive piece of information. Sasha didn’t generally enjoy gambling with other people’s money. But she also didn’t allow her clients to be pushed into making snap judgments.

“Okay. I don’t see any other option. I’m not prepared to accept an offer right now, so go ahead and call her.” She peeked at her watch. “We should go.”

She reached for her purse, but Sasha waved her off. "My treat."

She flipped over the bill and covered it with a ten. Then, she recalled Dana's tired, resigned eyes and the fact that she was working a double shift. She replaced the ten with a twenty and stood.

"After you."

27

Sasha followed Gella's VW bug up the long, sloping driveway that led from the road to Essiah Wheaton and Sheila Johnson's house. The driveway forked off to a small parking pad set in front of the house before continuing back to a garage structure. Gella took the fork and parked. Sasha did, as well.

The house was screened by a row of large, flowering bushes that began on either side of the low porch and curved around to the back. Sasha turned and looked down to the road. The location and landscaping afforded almost total privacy.

She joined Gella on the screened-in porch.

"Did you talk to the attorney?"

"No, which is perfect. I left a message explaining

that you and I are about to enter a meeting and can't be interrupted. I expressed interest in the concept of settling but said we really need to speak about specifics. If we haven't connected by noon, it would be bad form, bordering on misconduct, for her to withdraw the offer. And, don't worry—I'll be sure we don't connect by noon." She flashed her client a reassuring smile.

Gella rang the doorbell.

The faint sound of shoes clicking against a hard surface came from inside the house, growing louder. The door opened.

A tall woman wearing a black suit dress and black heels stood in the doorway. She was pale, but her hair was coiffed and her makeup was perfectly applied. Essiah Wheaton's widow looked more pulled together than Sasha felt.

It became clear almost immediately, though, that her composure was a veneer.

"Ms. Johnson? I'm Gella Pinkney. This is my ... uh ... attorney, Sasha McCandless-Connelly. We're so very sorry about Essiah's death."

Tears poured from the woman's eyes. She dabbed at them with a crumbled and twisted tissue that she had knotted around her right hand.

"Please, call me Sheila Anne. And come on in." Her

tremulous voice hinted at a southern twang. She ushered them off the porch.

Sasha followed Gella over the threshold and glanced around. The cabin-style house was considerably larger than it appeared from the outside. The entryway had a soaring, vaulted ceiling and exposed wooden beams and supports. The light-colored tile floor provided a contrast to all the dark woodwork. The entryway was casually decorated but devoid of personal touches. No framed pictures hung on the walls, no ceramic tchotchkes lined the shelves. The effect was homey, but not *home.*

"Was it just the two of you?" Sasha asked as Sheila Anne led them into a cozy den dominated by a tall stacked stone fireplace and wide hearth.

"Yes. We only met last fall." She raised her chin as if to ward off any disapproval. "We got married during the Christmas holidays. It was love at first sight."

Sasha smiled. "I was supposed to get married on New Year's Eve, myself." She hoped the common ground might put the widow at ease. The last thing she and Gella needed was a would-be plaintiff who was on the defensive from the outset.

"Supposed to? You didn't?" Curiosity won out, and Sheila Anne relaxed her shoulders slightly but perceptibly as she took a seat in the chair nearest the fireplace.

Sasha joined Gella on the leather couch. "We moved

it up a day. It's a long story." *Involving a thwarted attack by armed banditos at a Central American resort.* It was the kind of tale that could derail a conversation.

They lapsed into a long, oppressive silence.

Gella broke through the tension. She leaned forward, rested her elbows on her knees, and studied Sheila Anne's tear-stained face. "I'm sure your husband's death must've been quite a shock. Is someone staying with you?" Her voice was gentle but probing.

"No. We don't have any family nearby. We've only lived here since January." She twisted her fraying tissues in her hands.

"We met a waitress at the diner outside town—Dana. She seems to care about you. She wanted us to let you know she's praying for you and she'll come by to see you later," Gella offered.

"Dana's sweet. We're not really close, but her boyfriend and Essiah were tight. I guess ... he made friends more easily than I do. He fell in with a group of guys right away. I keep to myself. Work in the yard or read. I've always been a homebody."

She reached behind her, pulled a soft afghan down from the back of the chair, and wrapped it around herself.

Sasha glanced sidelong at Gella. This woman was in no shape to discuss any claims her dead husband might have against DoGiveThrive. She hoped Gella knew what to say next because this conversation veered much closer to a pastoral comfort situation than a discussion about liability.

Gella seemed to know what she was thinking. She nodded.

"I run a charity now, Sheila Anne, but I did attend divinity school. Would you like to pray together?"

The woman nodded her head. "I appreciate that, Miss Gella, yes, let's do that. My minister came by last night, and I know Essiah's with the Lord. I just ... I can't believe he's gone." Fresh tears filled her eyes and her shoulders shook.

Sasha, a lapsed Catholic, shifted in her seat awkwardly, feeling trapped. She popped to her feet.

"I'll get you a glass of water."

She hurried out of the room while Gella walked over and knelt beside Sheila Anne's chair. The two women bowed their heads.

She headed toward the back of the house. The kitchen was clean and cheerful with a white apron sink and a maple butcher block island. Pans hung from overhead. A red, orange, and yellow rag rug under a small, round table added a splash of cheerful color.

She opened and closed cabinets until she found the glasses. She filled one with water from the pitcher in

Sheila Anne's refrigerator then leaned against the counter, listening. Gella's voice rose and fell in a comforting cadence. The new widow sniffled.

She wandered around the kitchen to give them another moment. The back windows looked out over a small deck and an expansive yard.

Raised garden beds and a potting shed sat off to the left. The driveway curved around from the right and terminated at a weathered structure about fifty yards from the garden. Yellow crime scene tape crisscrossed the open bay door of the garage/barn.

She stared out the window and imagined the horror of discovering your husband's body in the backyard. A shiver shot up her spine.

She fought the temptation to pull out her phone and check for messages. She'd turned off her notifications after leaving the voicemail for Angela Washington. There was no point in checking now. She didn't care if the lawyer had gotten back to her yet. She was really interested in whether Connelly had tried to reach her.

If he had, she couldn't call him now, anyway, and that fact would drive her to distraction for the duration of this visit with Wheaton's widow.

And if he hadn't?

She pushed the thought from her mind.

She returned to the living room and placed the glass on the table at Sheila Anne's elbow.

"Thanks." She managed a wan smile.

"Don't mention it."

Gella shifted her position to include Sasha in the conversation. "Sheila Anne was just telling me how she and Essiah met."

"Oh?"

"Yeah." She lifted the glass with a shaky hand and took a sip. "We ended up at the same shelter after Harvey."

Sasha cocked her head to the side. "Hurricane Harvey?"

"Yeah, it was horrible. The storm destroyed both our towns. But, afterwards, we realized we never would've met if it hadn't happened. Essiah lived in an itty-bitty town near the Gulf Coast, and I lived about forty miles west of Houston. It was pure happenstance that we both ended up at the same church shelter in the Panhandle at the same time."

She gave a bewildered shake of her head at the events that had brought her and Essiah together.

The background explained Essiah's giving pattern. He'd been displaced by a hurricane. Once he was back on his feet, he must've wanted to lend a hand to people who'd suffered the same fate.

"What did Essiah do? I mean, where did he work?" Sasha asked.

Sheila's voice was high-pitched and fast when she answered. "I know this'll sound crazy, but he didn't. I mean, since we've been together. He said he worked in banking before. I guess he had some money saved up? After we relocated, he wanted to enjoy our time together for a while before we found jobs. We were living off his savings."

"Did he have life insurance, Sheila Anne?" Sasha kept her face blank.

Out of the corner of her eye, she saw Gella looking around the spacious, well-kept home. She suspected they were sharing the same unhappy thought: An out-of-work widow who just lost her sole source of income could make for a motivated plaintiff.

Sheila's red-rimmed eyes went wide. "Oh, gosh. I don't rightly know. I guess I'll have to stop in at the bank in town and go through the papers in his safe deposit box."

"You should definitely do that. And we know you have a great deal to do to make arrangements for Essiah. I imagine you're also working with the police?" Sasha said.

"Um, yeah. Well, the FBI, actually," she said in an offhand way, more focused on the unhappy tasks that lay ahead of her than on the specifics of the investigation into her husband's death.

But Sasha's antenna went up. "The FBI? Why?"

"I don't know. Nobody said. Or maybe they did? I don't remember, I was ... I guess, I was in shock."

Gella patted her arm. "That's perfectly understandable."

Sasha smoothed her expression. "Of course. It's just a bit unusual for the Federal Bureau of Investigation to get involved, even in a homicide investigation." Unless, of course, the homicide in question was related in some way to a federal operation, like, oh, say, an NCTC project.

Sheila Anne raised her shoulders and gave Sasha a helpless look.

Time to move on. "You and Essiah didn't have any problems with anyone?"

"Of course not. I mean, we've only lived here five months. We didn't make enemies."

"Maybe someone from your past?"

"The agents asked me all these questions. I was a preschool teacher back in Texas. I loved my students, my coworkers, my neighbors. My parents passed away years ago, and I'm an only child, so I don't have a big family, but I loved my life. If that dang hurricane hadn't hit, I'd still be in Blossom Creek teaching the days of the week song."

Gella and Sasha exchanged a glance.

"What about Essiah? Did he feel the same way about Texas?"

She drank some water and considered the question. "Not exactly. I mean, I don't rightly know. He didn't like to talk about ... before. He lost everything in the flooding. And he was like me. No brothers or sisters, his parents had passed. Once we started dating seriously, we decided it was time to look for a place to live. I figured we'd end up near Houston. But he found this place in the back of some magazine selling farms and ranches and talked me into it." She spread her arms wide and gestured around the room with a slightly dazed expression that suggested she wasn't quite sure how she ended up there.

"Sight unseen?"

She laughed. "Crazy, right? But, yeah. He made it sound like such an adventure, a new beginning, something we could share that would be just ours. I joked about Mars, you know, it sounded so alien, so foreign. But Essiah was like that. He was so enthusiastic and I guess I got caught up in it. He was right, though. I like it here." A half-smile played across her lips then died as quickly as it had bloomed.

The whirlwind move and fresh start might have seemed like a romantic leap to Sheila Anne. But to Sasha, it smacked of a man who was running from his past. And now he was dead, which led her to believe his past had caught up with him. The only question she wanted to answer was whether Asher Morgan's little stunt was why Essiah Wheaton's old life had crashed into his new one with such disastrous results?

Judging by the worry lines creasing Gella's forehead and the anxious shadow in her eyes, her client had reached the same conclusion and was wondering the same thing.

"Did you know Essiah made several generous donations to hurricane victims?" Sasha asked.

Sheila Anne blinked. "I'm not surprised. He was very kind that way. But, we never talked about it. The hurricane ... it affected us, you know? Even though it brought us together and something good came out of it, it caused such suffering. We didn't like to talk about it."

"I can understand that. But, Sasha's right. He gave quite a bit of money to projects devoted to helping hurricane victims. As I mentioned on the phone, my company works to connect donors like Essiah with folks who are in need—"

"Yeah, I looked you up online after we talked. It seems like a good thing you do." She hesitated. "But I ...

right now, I'm not in a position to give anything. I don't even know how much money we have. I've got an appointment with Essiah's guy at the bank after I meet with the funeral director." She smiled sheepishly.

"Oh, sweetie, no, we're not here asking for a donation. Goodness. No, the reason we wanted to talk to you ... well, Sasha, maybe you could explain it better?" Gella assured the woman then turned to Sasha.

"Sure. The reason DoGiveThrive was trying to reach your husband was to let him know that there'd been a data breach and his account was affected."

"A breach? Like, a hack? Did they get his credit card number? Should I call the bank?"

"No, nothing like that. So, part of DoGiveThrive's promise to its users is to keep their identities secret. They guarantee anonymous donations, and the recipients remain anonymous, too."

Sheila Anne nodded slowly. "Okay? Then, what was leaked?"

"Your husband's name and your zip code."

She furrowed her forehead. "What else?"

"Nothing else. That was the extent of the leak. A list of donor names and zip codes was posted to the internet for a period of time lasting between eight and twelve hours from Sunday night into Monday morning."

She blinked. “That’s it? His name was on the internet?”

“Well, yes. But we wanted to assure him—and now, you—that the company takes the breach very seriously and is taking steps to ensure it never happens again.”

“Okay. Listen, you both seem like nice women. And I might be missing something here, but I think y’all may be overreacting just a touch.”

Sasha’s mind raced as she tried to balance her duty to DoGiveThrive with her duty of candor to a woman who may have been affected by the leak. She couldn’t blurt out the possibility that Essiah was dead because of the leak. And if that was true, didn’t it mean the NCTC was behind his death? And if *that* was true, this whole mess was a matter of national security. Which would explain the FBI’s involvement. Her head spun, and she really, really wished she could pick up the phone and ask Connelly for advice right now.

Gella and Sheila Anne were staring at her.

She smiled tightly, pulled herself together, and managed an answer, “DoGiveThrive would rather over-react than sweep this under the rug. In fact, we’ve filed a complaint against the man responsible for the leak and his employer.”

Sheila Anne glanced at her watch. “I don’t mean to

hustle you out of here, but I have an appointment at the funeral home. Thanks for coming up but—"

"We got a request from the government," Gella blurted. "They wanted to know whether a list of names appeared in our database. We refused to turn the names over, citing privacy concerns. But your husband's name was on that list."

Sasha watched the woman's face closely. Gella's bombshell seemed to have little effect.

"The government was asking about Essiah? That's odd. But, you know, a lot of people got lost in the system after the hurricanes displaced them. It took me forever to get my mail sorted out. Maybe it was just something like that?"

"Maybe," Sasha said weakly.

Gella caught her eye. She shrugged. She wasn't going to force feed the woman a narrative that painted DoGiveThrive as responsible for her husband's death.

She stood. "We've taken up more than enough of your time. Thank you for talking to us. And, again, I'm so, so sorry about your loss."

At the mention of her husband's death, Sheila Anne's eyes overflowed again as the three of them made their way toward the front door. Her overworked tissue disintegrated in her hand.

Gella plucked a fresh one from a packet in her purse

and pressed it into the widow's hand. "May I go with you to the funeral home, Sheila Anne? That's not something you should do alone."

"Oh, I couldn't ask you to do that."

"You didn't. I offered."

Sheila Anne managed a wobbly smile. "If you mean that, I'd be grateful for your company."

"It's settled then."

Sasha coughed. "What about your meeting in Ohio?" she asked in an undertone.

"I'll reschedule. Can you really put off that attorney?"

"Consider it done."

They reached the front door. Sasha spotted a manila envelope lying face down on the floor in front of the threshold, as if someone had slipped it under the door. She bent and retrieved it.

"Looks like you got some mail."

She handed the envelope to Sheila Anne, who flipped it over and gasped. Her face was white and her eyes were filled with a mixture of dread and fear.

"What's wrong?"

She thrust the envelope at Sasha, her hand shaking wildly. Gella wrapped an arm around the widow's shoulder.

Sasha looked at the front of the envelope. The words

"OPEN IN THE EVENT OF MY DEATH" were written across the front.

"That's Essiah's handwriting."

Sasha's pulse fluttered. She tried to hand the envelope back to Sheila Anne. "You should open it."

She shook her head. "I can't. One of you do it."

Sasha's eyes met Gella's.

"Here, let me."

She handed the envelope to her client.

She and Sheila Anne both leaned in over Gella's shoulders and watched her carefully open the envelope and remove several sheets of paper.

A printed note lay on the top of the stack. It was brief and to the point:

These are photographs of the man who killed me.

Sheila Anne swayed on her feet. Gella dropped the papers and steadied her with both hands.

Sasha crouched and gathered up the papers. She was about to tell Sheila Anne to call the FBI when she turned over the first picture. The words died in her throat.

She was holding a picture of her husband. Connelly was peering through some bushes looking up at the house she was currently standing in. The photograph was grainy. It had been taken at night, in the rain, and from a distance. But it was unmistakably a picture of Connelly.

A time and date were printed on the bottom of the page. The photograph was taken two nights ago—the last time she'd seen him. When he left abruptly after dinner.

Her stomach lurched as she paged through the rest of the photos. Connelly in profile, standing under a tree. Then a close-up of his familiar face. His square jaw set in a determined line. His gray eyes fierce as he stared at someone—or something—off camera with a look she didn't recognize. A hard, cold, deadly look.

She willed herself not to sink to her knees. She breathed through her nose as slowly as she could to avoid hyperventilating. She had to keep it together. Had to. Her heart thudded, and the rushing blood in her ears sounded like the roar of the ocean.

Gella remained focused on Sheila Anne, who still looked as if she might faint.

Sasha croaked. Her throat was bone dry. She worked up enough saliva to speak and tried again. "Do you want me to take care of these pictures?"

Sheila Anne didn't respond.

"Why don't you let Sasha handle that envelope for you? She'll know what to do," Gella suggested.

The stricken widow stared at Sasha with wide, terrified eyes for a moment then nodded her agreement.

Sasha stuffed the pages back into the envelope and ran, stumbling out of the house before Sheila Anne could change her mind.

28

Leo smashed his hand down to silence the blaring alarm clock. He rolled over onto his back and opened his eyes. It took a moment to realize where he was, and why.

He eyeballed the time display. It was nine thirty on the dot.

He stood, cracked his back, and padded to the bathroom in his boxers and undershirt. He used the complimentary toothpaste and his finger to brush his teeth. Then he splashed cold water on his face and ran a hand over the two days' growth on his chin and cheeks.

He fumbled through the pockets of the pants he'd worn last night until he found his phone.

His finger hovered over his contact list. He wanted,

more than anything, to call Sasha. But he needed to call Hank first.

He raked his hands through his hair while he waited for the call to connect.

"Hi. Tell me you've got something for me." Hank answered halfway through the first ring.

"I'm working on it."

"That's not good enough."

"What's that supposed to mean?" he bristled.

"What it means is the Bureau asserted jurisdiction over the investigation and—"

"Why would they do that?"

"It's procedure, according to Ingrid. Even though a no questions kill order is designed to provide maximum cover for the ordering agency—"

"Cover for the agency? Screw the operative, right?" Hot anger flared in his gut.

"How 'bout you stop interrupting me?" Hank's voice was cool, impersonal.

"Sorry."

"Like I was saying, despite the fact that the order gives the agency complete deniability, Project Storm Chaser authorized the Bureau to step in and make sure the investigation is resolved in a desirable manner."

"So, in plain English, the task force is ready to perpetrate a cover up if necessary."

"In a nutshell. Don't act surprised. You've been around long enough to know how the sausage is made. And, while you're not the intended beneficiary, any sanitation work they do will ultimately protect you, too."

He rolled his neck to work out the kinks and release some of his building irritation. "Okay, that's fair. But in this case, it's a problem. Because any brick agent worth his salt will take one look at Essiah Wheaton and know it wasn't a government job."

"It's already happened. Ingrid's asking questions. Give me something."

"I've worked my way into a group of Wheaton's buddies. I'm meeting up with them again in about an hour. I'll come away with something solid from that. Can you buy me the rest of the morning?"

"Leo, you know I will. But I need something to buy it *with*."

He squeezed his eyes shut and flipped through his mental notes from the conversations with Wheaton's crew.

"Sheila Anne Johnson."

"Who's she?" Leo heard the familiar zing of excitement in Hank's voice.

"Wheaton's wife. Another native Texan, but from a different part of the state. His pals said they met in August or September, were married by December, and moved to Mars at the end of January. That's a little unusual, don't you think?"

"Maybe, maybe not. After all, *'the heart wants what it wants.'*"

"What, are you listening to pop with Brianna now?"

"What? No, that's an Emily Dickinson quote, you philistine."

"If you say so, old man."

They were both laying on the shtick a little heavier than was strictly necessary, but it was better than letting a wall of distrust spring up between them. Hank was, in many ways, his partner more than his boss. And the worst feeling out in the field was the suspicion that your partner didn't have your back.

He winced at that thought. The obvious corollary cut a bit too close: The worst feeling in a marriage was the suspicion that your partner didn't have your back.

"I'll feed her name to Ingrid and run it through some databases, see if anything pops."

"Thanks. I'll call you with an update after I meet these guys. Don't call me unless you have to, okay?"

"Understood."

"And Hank?"

"Yeah?"

"Can you check on Sasha for me?"

Hank made a sound that was half-sigh, half-groan.

"What?"

"She was pretty fired up yesterday. I don't want to have to lie to her or evade her questions. Can't you just ... I dunno, text her?"

"Gee, I wonder why you're still single."

Hank snorted. "Let's see if we make any progress with this Johnson woman. Maybe you can wrap things up this morning in time to meet Sasha for a late lunch and make up for the past couple of days."

"Maybe."

"Stay sharp."

"Right."

He ended the call and spent a few minutes scrolling through pictures of Finn and Fiona on his phone's camera roll. He smiled at the images, but his chest cavity felt as if it were being squeezed in a vise—he missed his kids so much that the thought of them gave him an actual, physical heartache. He shut down the phone and found his clothes.

The clerk at the check-in desk had mentioned a free continental breakfast bar in the lobby, and he had time to spare. He wasn't quite sure what brunch at a dive bar would entail, so he figured he might as well grab a bite before he headed to Mugsy's.

29

"You're not going to believe this, but that guy, the fed, is staying at the same hotel as us."

Fletch pulled the phone away from his ear.

Was Chuck joking? What a dumb thing to joke about.

"Are you serious? How small is that town?"

"Smaller than small. And I'm dead serious. What should we do?"

Fletch watched from the veranda as his pool guy crouched by the water and took out a case of testing strips.

"What am I, your babysitter? Did you get the pictures developed?"

"Yeah, of course." Chuck said in a sore voice. "We

drove over to Wheaton's house this morning and slipped the envelope under the front door."

"In broad daylight? Was she home?"

These two geniuses were going to give him an ulcer —unless his growing suspicion that Melody Lynn was sneaking around with his pool boy like a caricature of a desperate housewife did him in first.

"Relax. She was home, but she had company. There were two cars in the driveway. I watched through the binoculars from behind a row of trees while Marcus took care of the envelope. She was in her living room with two other ladies the whole time, crying and talking. None of them noticed him."

"Hmm." Fletch's attention wandered from Marcus's story as his wife walked into the kitchen wearing a hot pink two-piece bathing suit and some oversized sunglasses like she thought she was Audrey Hepburn. "Hang on a sec," he instructed Marcus.

Then he covered the phone with his hand and yelled into the kitchen, "Hey, hon, you can't go swimming right now. Phillip's out there checking the levels."

She slid open the glass door and joined him on the covered sun porch. She pushed the sunglasses up to the crown of her head and squinted toward the pool.

"That's not Phillip, silly. That's Neo."

"Neo? What in the hell kind of name is Neo?"

She shrugged. “It looks hot out there. Did you offer him some lemonade or an iced coffee?”

“No, I didn’t offer him any cold drinks, Melly. I’m paying him with American currency to do a job. He can buy his own freaking lemonade.”

She rolled her eyes and tottered off on her kitten-heeled sandals in the direction of the pool boy.

He clenched his fist and returned his attention to his other, more pressing problem.

“I’m back.”

“So what should we do?”

“I imagine this Sheila Anne’ll go straight to the cops with the envelope. All you need to do is keep an eye on the G-man until he leaves town or the local authorities catch up with him.”

“So, follow him?”

Fletch bit back his first, sarcastic response. And his second.

“Yes,” he said simply.

“Got it. Tail him, but don’t engage.”

“Right.”

“What if I have Marcus call the cops, you know, anonymously? Maybe in an hour or so? He could tip them off that this guy was seen near Wheaton’s house before he was murdered and give them his location to speed things along?”

Fletch smiled to himself. "Now that's the kind of strategy I expect from you, Chuck. That's brilliant. Yes, do that."

"Roger that. I'll call you when we have an update."

"Good."

Fletcher ended the call, narrowed his eyes, and settled back on the chaise lounge to watch his wife flirt with Neo. He couldn't quite tell if the guy was just really tan or if he was brown.

Either way, Melody had better watch her step, he told himself. *Otherwise, Chuck would have another job waiting for him when he got back to town.*

30

Within seconds after pulling out of Shelia Anne's driveway, Sasha realized she was shaking too badly to drive. She pulled over to the shoulder, parked, and turned off the engine.

She pressed her palms flat against the tops of her thighs and focused on her breathing with an intensity she'd last felt during active labor with the twins.

Now, as then, her efforts didn't stop her from vomiting. She jerked open the door and lurched out onto the berm just in time to lose her coffee in the gravel and not all over her front seat.

She leaned against the hood of the car until she stopped heaving then she wiped her mouth with the back of her hand and took a series of deep, greedy breaths to fill her lungs with fresh air.

Once she felt steadier on her feet, she stretched across the front seat of the station wagon and rummaged through her glove box.

Parenting twins was like being an Eagle Scout, or a big firm associate for that matter. Prepare for every contingency. That was her motto.

She re-emerged from the car with a package of natural face wipes, a travel toothbrush and toothpaste, and a lukewarm mini-bottle of water.

Once she was minty-fresh and sparkling clean again, she slid back behind the wheel of the car but didn't start the engine.

She sat stock still and upright and stared through the windshield at the undulating hills in front of her, studiously refusing to so much as glance at the envelope resting on her passenger seat.

After a long moment, she asked herself the question that had turned her stomach:

Did she believe her husband had sat across the table from her and shared a meal, then walked the dog, and left her home with their children to drive out here and kill someone else's husband?

No. Her heart answered instantly and emphatically. Not Connelly. Not her husband, lover, best friend.

Her brain piped up. He took his gun out of the safe, left in the middle of a rainstorm, and hasn't come back.

Oh, and that is him skulking around Essiah Wheaton and Sheila Anne Johnson's backyard in those pictures. And someone killed Essiah Wheaton.

Her stomach lurched again. She pressed her palm flat against it, even though she knew it was completely empty now.

There must be a reasonable explanation.

Sure. Like, maybe you're married to a special agent who works for a government agency so secretive that you're not allowed to know what it's called. And maybe, just maybe, this shady agency engages in activities the government would rather keep quiet. Perhaps, say, at the direction of the NCTC.

The logic was airtight and seductive. It made so much sense.

No.

She covered her ears with her hands even though that did nothing to silence the words considering they were inside her head.

She exhaled and watched the landscape blur like a watercolor painting as her eyes filled with tears.

One of two things was true. She was either losing her mind or coming to grips with the fact that she was married to a stranger.

Her heart whispered. *Or, third option, Connelly's being set up.*

She sat with that idea for a moment. It could explain why he'd disappeared. He might be trying to clear his name. She glanced at the envelope. And that note—who types a farewell note to his beloved and, not only that, leaves such a sterile message: *These are photographs of the man who killed me.* No my darling Sheila Anne? No, Love, Essiah? It smelled funny.

Or you're deluding yourself to avoid reality, her brain hissed.

She closed her eyes and called up an image of her husband. His clear gray eyes, half-smile, sharp cheekbones, and thick, spiky black hair—with one small patch of gray right behind his left ear, which, she was convinced, he had no idea existed. The man who stayed by her side after she watched a woman die at her feet. Who proposed to her, not once, but twice. Who never doubted her, who never backed down from a threat. Who cooked all their meals, diapered their children, and taught them lullabies in halting Vietnamese. Who donated part of his liver to his estranged father and then turned that same man in to the authorities for murder.

No. Not Connelly.

She dug her phone out of her bag and placed the call she had to make.

"Hello?" He answered halfway through the first ring.

"It's me."

"Uh—"

"Don't. Hank, why am I holding a set of photographs of my absent husband lurking in the backyard of a man who was murdered yesterday?"

"What?" Hank's confusion seemed genuine, but then she doubted she knew him as well as she thought.

"Let's try it this way. Did Connelly kill Essiah Wheaton? And if so, was it at your direction?"

"I can't answer these questions."

"That's not a no."

"It's not a yes," he countered.

"Hank, I don't have time for this BS."

"Where are you?"

"Irrelevant."

"Are you with Leo?"

"Are you kidding? I haven't seen him for two days. Why is that? Where is he? What have you told him to do?" She kept her voice as level as she could manage, but she could hear a note of rising panic as she spat rapid-fire questions at a man she'd always considered a friend—no, more than a friend. A rock.

Hank answered her in a patient tone. "You know I can't tell you anything, sweetheart."

"Don't call me that."

"Okay. I'm sorry. Look, I don't know anything about

any photographs. Why don't you come over to my place, and we can talk this through?"

An ugly thought popped into her mind. Was he stalling? Keeping her on the line so he could pinpoint her location? She was certain he had the technical capability to do it.

"I have to go. If you talk to my husband, let him know that if he didn't kill that man, someone's trying to make it look like he did."

She hung up and stared down at the phone in her hands. Was there someone else she could call? Naya? Will?

The only person she wanted to talk to—needed to talk to—was Connelly. Together, they could figure out a way to fix this. They'd gotten out of tighter spots more than once.

Her finger hesitated just above his name. She should call him. She had to call him. But the fact that he'd left her on her own stung. He clearly didn't want her help.

31

Leo was walking across Mugsy's parking lot when his phone rang. To his considerable horror, he'd just surreptitiously smelled his armpit. He assumed the dress code for a wake at a dive bar was fairly loose, but he also figured wearing the same clothes he'd worn last night was pushing the envelope.

At the sound of the ringtone he'd assigned to Hank, he forgot about his hygiene issue.

"Did you get something on Sheila Johnson?"

"Hi, yourself. No. But we have a problem."

"Hank, I already have a problem, remember? This new one is all yours."

"Sorry, that's not how it works."

Leo sighed. "Look, I'm about to go into a biker bar. I

need to get my head on straight first. So why don't you just tell me what's going on so we can get on with it.'

"You're not going to like it."

He didn't like any of this, but he wasn't about to express that thought to his boss.

"Okay."

"Somehow—and, no, before you ask, I don't know how—somehow, your wife got her hands on a series of photographs of you that someone took the night you cased Wheaton's house."

"I knew that wasn't a freaking raccoon."

"Yeah, well, whoever was out there is claiming you killed Wheaton. That's obviously something we could mop up. Except ..."

"Except the field agent assigned to the case is going to say Wheaton was strangled, and not by a pro, right?" A boulder landed in his stomach as he forced out the words.

"Right. It wasn't a clean kill. I mean, no fingerprints, no DNA. But the technique ... strictly amateur hour. But that's not the real issue."

"Oh?" He stopped just outside Mugsy's metal doors. "What's the real issue?"

"The real issue is that Sasha is hopping mad. She's running around with those pictures, and I have no idea where she is. I tried to geo-locate and triangulate the call, but she hung up too soon."

"Crap."

"Double crap."

"And she's got it in her head that you're being railroaded."

"Well, I kind of am."

"Yeah, but for a crime you were *supposed* to commit," Hank pointed out.

"Details."

"I don't even want to think about the paperwork I'm going to have to do."

Leo'd had enough years of government service under his belt to know that there was more than a seed of truth in Hank's gallows humor. He hurried to change the subject.

"Did you try Naya?"

"Yeah. She said Sasha had a meeting outside the office and that your in-laws have the kids. Maybe you should call them?"

"That's a dead end. She wouldn't tell them anything that might make them worry."

They shared a heavy silence.

Finally, Hank said, "I'll reach out to Ingrid. I already have a rush on the Sheila Anne Johnson search. I guess all we can do is hope your wife doesn't do anything rash."

"Sasha? Rash? Is the sky blue?"

Leo hung up to the sound of Hank's resigned chuckling and put his unpredictable, unstoppable wife out of his mind. He had to focus. He pushed the door open.

He didn't notice the two men in the rental car who were watching from the parking lot of the gas station next door.

32

Fletcher was nailing his wife in the pool house when the call came in. He heard it. But he had other priorities, like reminding Melody Lynn that she was married to a virile, successful white man. He was marking his territory, so he just had to hope that Chuck and Marcus would figure out their situation on their own.

When he was sated, and Melly was snuggled into the crook of his arm snoring softly, he reached for the phone with his free hand and played the message Chuck had left him:

Fletch, he's going into a biker bar. You know, Wheaton used to ride. I'm not sure this is the right call, but I don't wanna lose him, and I can't send Marcus in alone, so we're going to give it a couple minutes, then we're both going in.

With any luck, he'll nurse a brew, and we can call the cops to come pick him up here. For the Brotherhood, For Purity and Glory!"

It was the Heritage Brotherhood's rallying cry that would haunt him afterward. It would make him wonder what would have happened if he would've rolled off Melody long enough to take the call and give Chuck some direction.

33

Sasha was dead-eyed, drained, and dehydrated from crying and barfing when she reached the short commercial drag that led to the on-ramp to the highway.

She almost missed the turn for the gas station, which would have been a problem, since her fuel light had been on ever since she'd left Sheila Johnson's place. She swerved hard and yanked the wheel when she realized she was passing the entrance to the gas station. She bumped up over the curb and winced as metal rubbed up against concrete.

Connelly loved to tease her about the battle scars her station wagon sported.

Then she thought of Connelly and winced even

harder. What if he wasn't around to laugh at the yellow racing stripes her car seemed to acquire whenever she had to park near a pole in a tight garage?

She hopped out and swiped her credit card through the reader. As she filled the tank, cursing the Commonwealth of Pennsylvania and its astronomical fuel prices, she noted the two dudes in the silver Celica that screamed 'rental car.'

It was their lack of attention that caught hers. She was the only other person in the lot, but the guys didn't seem to register her presence. They sat motionless, staring hard at the biker bar next door as if it were their job. She glanced over to see what had them so transfixed.

That's when she spotted her husband's SUV in the parking lot.

Her heart jumped out of her chest and landed in her throat. Connelly was in that bar. She almost hurtled herself over the cement barrier that separated the two businesses.

She stopped herself, got into the car, and started the engine. She eased out into the travel lane for a few dozen feet then turned into the bar's parking lot.

She parked in the spot to the left of Connelly's SUV, shoved the envelope into her bag, and pasted a smile on face. She flipped her sunshade down and checked her nonexistent makeup in the lighted mirror on the reverse of the shade.

She looked exactly how she'd expect a single mother of three-year-old twins who hadn't slept in two nights and recently puked on the side of the road to look.

Perhaps charming her way into the bar was out of the question, she thought as she snapped the shade up. She peeked inside her wallet and counted six twenties. If nothing else, she ought to be able to buy her way in.

She shrugged out of her suit jacket, slung her bag over her shoulder, and marched toward the door, resisting the urge to shoot the bird at the guys watching from the gas station lot.

She rapped on the metal door and tried to still her pulse. It was fluttering so quickly that she could feel it under her right eyelid—a condition she'd last experienced during the bar exam fifteen years ago.

"This is bananas," she told herself.

She agreed wholeheartedly with her own assessment, yet here she was.

A handwritten note affixed to the door read 'CLOSED FOR PRIVATE WAKE.'

Wake?

So she banged her fist against the door again. She kept pounding until the side of her hand ached.

The door creaked open an inch. A bloodshot eye appeared in the opening.

"What?"

"Uh, I'm a friend of Sheila Anne's?" She said the words as a question, but they functioned as a password.

The door swung inward and she hurried inside.

The bar was crowded, smoky, and loud. In other words, it was everything she'd been avoiding for more than a decade.

She squared her shoulders and plunged into the crowd.

"Hey, I know you," a willowy brunette hollered before throwing back a shot.

She registered that she knew the woman, too. Dana. The waitress from the diner.

"Pete grew a heart and let me leave—he's covering my shift himself," Dana explained.

Sasha assumed Pete must be the woman's manager. She nodded distractedly and scanned the room. Where the devil was Connelly?

"You looking for Sheila Anne?" Dana asked. "I'm not sure she's coming. This isn't really her crowd."

"Sure," she said absently.

Through the sea of people, she spotted Connelly shouldering his way toward the back of the room. She pushed through the bodies, making a beeline for him.

He glanced around, eased open a metal door, and slipped inside.

Where was he going?

34

Sasha hesitated just outside the windowless door, unsure if she should follow her husband inside. She turned to check if anyone was paying attention to her. Just then two men walked into the bar. She narrowed her eyes. They were the guys from the gas station. And they were scanning the room intently. Searching for someone. Quite possibly the same someone she was here to see.

She yanked the door open and hurried into the back room.

Six men wearing black leather jackets turned to look at her. Based on their attire, she figured them for the motorcycle buddies Sheila Anne had mentioned. The seventh man wasn't wearing a motorcycle jacket, but he was wearing a shocked expression.

"What are you doing here?"

"We need to talk. Now."

He nodded. "That's fair. C.J., is there somewhere quiet where we can talk?"

The guy called C.J. pointed his thumb toward the back of the room. "The locker room is through that door. Who's the girl?"

Sasha folded her arms across her chest and waited to hear how he'd answer.

"She's my wife."

"In that case, good luck, pal. Because she looks madder than a bag full of hornets."

She flashed Connelly a tight smile as she walked through the cluster of men. The guy closest to the locker room held the door open for her. Connelly followed behind her and the guy holding the door gave him a sympathetic pat on the shoulder.

"You seem to have made friends quickly," she observed as the door clicked shut behind him.

"They're an interesting group of guys." He crossed the room and stood close, gazing down at her with an unreadable expression. "It's good to see you. I've missed you ... and the kids ... so much."

"Could've fooled me. Did you lose your phone?"

"Sasha, I'm sorry." He cupped her chin with one

hand and tilted her face up so she was staring into his eyes. "I didn't have a choice."

She turned her head to the side to dislodge his hand. "We can talk about this later. Right now, you have a bigger problem."

"I didn't kill Essiah Wheaton." He searched her face. "Do you believe me?"

"Yeah, I do."

He exhaled. "Thank you."

"But someone's trying to pin his murder on you." She dug the envelope out of her bag and handed it to him. "Go ahead, take a look."

She watched his face as he read the brief letter then slowly flipped through the photos, examining each one closely before turning to the next.

"All these pictures show was that I was at Wheaton's place two nights ago. But he was killed yesterday while I was sitting in the Houston airport waiting for my flight."

"Hang on. You went to Texas? What's going on, Connelly? Why did the NCTC send you to spy on Essiah and Sheila in the first place?"

He blinked. "I have a couple questions for you, too, you know. What are you doing here? How do you know Wheaton and Sheila Anne Johnson?"

She made a low, irritated noise in her throat.

"Remember my client with the data leak? The NCTC had a contractor send an information request?"

"Sure, I remember. And you had some theory that the leak was related to the request."

She didn't particularly care for his dismissive tone, but she forced herself not to get snappish. As betrayed and confused as she felt, she realized they really needed to work together if they were going to clear his name.

"Well, my *theory* is borne out by the fact that one of the names on the list Sentinel Solution Systems sent was Essiah Wheaton's. *And* his name and zip code were included in the leaked data. He was an extremely generous donor—mainly to causes related to the three big hurricanes that hit last year. My client was trying to call him to let him know his name had been published on the internet, but she never had the opportunity to talk to him. Last night, she spoke to Sheila Anne, who told her he'd been murdered."

He frowned at her, tugging on his right ear. "What's going on here? None of this makes any sense."

"Look, I shared what I know with you. If you tell me why you're so interested in Essiah Wheaton, maybe we can figure out who did kill him—together."

"It's not that easy. My information is classified."

"I'm really mad at you. Furious, actually. But I'm making an effort here. If you're just going to hide behind your national security BS, then I'm not sure why I'm bothering." She dug her fingernails into her palms and focused on the sting to keep her temper from boiling over.

"It's not BS. Wheaton was the subject of an active Joint Terrorism Task Force investigation. And, I'm sorry, but that's literally all I can tell you."

It was plenty.

"Well, your task force got it wrong. Essiah Wheaton wasn't a terrorist."

To her surprise, he nodded in agreement. "I think you're right. That's why I was in Texas—I was trying to get some better background on him. But the man was an enigma."

"That squares with what his wife said. His town was hit hard by Hurricane Harvey; so was hers. It sounded like he lost everything, and he didn't have any family. They were both staying at the same emergency shelter and fell in love. With nothing left in Texas, he found the farmette for sale in Mars and they moved up here. On a whim, basically."

"Or he was running from someone."

"I thought we just established that he wasn't a terrorist. Why would he be on the run from the government?"

"Not the government. Somehow he got mixed up with a group called the Heritage Brotherhood."

"White supremacists?"

"Yeah, of the violent variety."

"That name's familiar." She searched her memory. "Hmm, interesting ..."

He raised an eyebrow. "Care to share?"

"You know how I said Mr. Wheaton made several generous donations to hurricane victims?"

"Yeah, so?"

"He only ever made one donation that wasn't hurricane-related. It was to a group called Standing United. He gave them a thousand dollars for an anti-racism campaign after that campus riot in Georgia."

"Okay. So?"

"So the riot was supposed to be a unity rally organized by none other than the Heritage Brotherhood, who ended up suing Standing United. Coincidence?"

He snorted. She smiled. They shared the same opinion about coincidences—-mainly, that they didn't exist.

"Wheaton had a history with the Heritage Brotherhood, for sure. But there's no way he was a member."

"Right."

"It's good to have confirmation but that doesn't change the fact that somebody strangled him and there's probably an all-points bulletin advising local law enforcement to be on the lookout for me."

She shook her head. "I let Sheila Anne think I would give the pictures to the police. Obviously, I haven't."

"Why not?"

"Because you didn't kill anybody."

He exhaled. "It's good to be on the same side. Now we just have to figure out who *did* kill him."

She thought of the two men who'd been watching the bar. "I might have a couple suspects for you."

"You're just full of surprises, aren't you?"

He closed the small distance between them and gazed at her with an expression she knew well. He was about to kiss her. She saw it in the tilt of his chin, the softness in his eyes.

Her body was already responding, arching toward him. Her hands ready to come together behind his head while her fingers danced through his thick hair.

Really? After that stunt, you're just going to fall into his arms?

She froze as the voice in her head scolded her.

He must have noticed her sudden stiffness, because his eyebrows came together in a question.

"What's—?"

The door banged open and hit the wall.

They leapt apart.

Sasha whirled around, fists raised, heart thumping, ready for a fight. She cursed herself for not paying closer attention to her bad feeling about those guys from the parking lot.

"Oh, gosh! I'm sorry, I didn't know anyone was in here!" Dana, the waitress, ducked her head and gave them a sheepish smile.

Leo turned to glare at the interloper. He'd been *this* close to kissing his wife. And now Sasha was in a fighting stance. Mood ruined.

"Oops." The woman tripped over her own feet. Her arm flew out and she braced herself against the wall.

"Dana?" She was the waitress from the diner.

"Hey, it's you." She turned from him to Sasha. "And you. 'Member I told you I had another customer with three-year-old twins? This is him! How weird is that? You guys know each other or something?"

"We're married," Sasha told her in a tone that suggested she wasn't entirely thrilled about it at the moment.

"Ooooh. That makes sense. Listen, sorry to interrupt. I need to grab something from Essiah's locker and I'll be out of your hair."

"Essiah Wheaton has a locker here?"

"A bunch of the guys do. Bill, the owner, lets them

keep their games here so they don't have to lug them around in their saddlebags," Leo explained.

Sasha stared at him. "How much time have you spent here?"

He laughed sadly. "Too much."

She held his eyes for a moment then turned back to the waitress.

"So you're cleaning out Essiah's locker for Sheila Anne?"

"Not exactly. Essiah made C.J. promise that if anything ever happened to him, he'd take his Battleship game and give it to the police. Isn't that super weird?"

He had to agree that it was an odd last request.

"C.J.'s your boyfriend, right?" he confirmed.

"Yeah." She swayed and ended up propping herself against the wall.

Sasha narrowed her eyes. "How many shots have you done?"

Dana shook her head. "Just the one. I'm not drunk."

"But you worked all night. Have you slept?"

"Nah. I'll take a nap after I drop the game off for C.J. Now *he's* in no condition to drive. He was up all night drinking with your husband and some of the guys."

Sasha arched a brow and gave Leo a look.

He smiled innocently.

She shook her head and turned back to Dana, "Have you eaten anything?"

"Uh … I can't remember. Maybe some fries last night."

Sasha took the waitress by the arm and led her to a metal folding chair in the corner. "Sit."

Dana sat.

"Listen, you're not in any shape to drive either. Yeah, I heard you, you only did one shot."

She kept talking as the woman opened her mouth to protest. "But a fast influx of alcohol on no sleep and no food is going to hit you harder than you think. And the sleep deprivation alone makes it dangerous for you to drive. You just sit here and rest. We'll make sure Essiah's Battleship game gets into the proper hands."

Like hell we will, he thought. Then the words she'd actually said registered and he focused on keeping his expression neutral. His tricky lawyer wife had no intention of handing over whatever was in that box to the local police.

"She's right," he weighed in.

His opinion turned out to be unnecessary because the waitress was already slumped over in the chair, sleeping.

"That was fast."

"I hope she doesn't fall out of the chair and hit her

head," Sasha fretted.

He lifted the woman as if she were a ragdoll and laid her gently on the carpet. She didn't react. "There. Now all we need to do is figure out which locker is Essiah's."

He turned and surveyed the row of lockers with a frown. Sasha bent and removed a small key from Dana's hand.

"Probably seventeen." She flashed him the key. A number was painted on the key's silver head with red nail polish.

She stepped over Dana and inserted the key in Locker 17. She stretched up on her toes and removed an armload of stuff.

"Here, let me help you."

She handed him half the pile and they spread it all out on a low wooden bench that was situated in the middle of the floor between the two sets of lockers. A jacket; a set of Magic: The Gathering cards; a case of poker chips; a battered cardboard Scrabble box; and a Battleship box that was in decent shape.

While Sasha checked out the Battleship game, he gathered up the rest of Wheaton's belongings and returned them to the locker. He relocked the door and pressed the key into Dana's outstretched hand then wrapped her fingers around it. She moaned and shifted but didn't wake up.

"We should get out of here," he whispered.

Sasha nodded but her attention was on the contents of the box. She'd lifted the gray, plastic cases that housed the pegs and the pegboards out of the box to reveal a stack of papers.

"Look at this." She passed him the top sheet.

He skimmed it.

If you're reading this, I'm dead.

If the circumstances of my death were suspicious, please look to a man named Fletcher Lee Holden and a group called the Heritage Brotherhood, located in Texas. Holden vowed to kill me, and I have no doubt he will if he ever finds me.

You'll see why if you review the enclosed documents. I'm sorry for putting them in code, but I don't want anyone to stumble on this information by accident and find themselves in the crosshairs with Holden like I did.

If you value your life, you'll proceed with caution.

Sincerely,

Essiah Wheaton

"There's a code?"

She spread out a handful of papers. "It's all digits, just row after row of numbers."

"No key, right?"

She shot him a look. “What do you think?”

He realized it was a stupid question, but a guy could hope.

“That’s okay. The data analysts’ll be able to crack it in their sleep.”

She returned the game cases to the box and replaced the lid. Then she shuffled the papers into a tidy stack, plucked the note out of his hand, and placed it on the top of the pile.

“What analysts would those be?” she asked in a conversational tone while carefully sliding the papers into the pale blue leather bag she used to transport everything from her laptop to massive client files and emergency changes of clothes for the twins. She tucked the game under her arm.

“The NCTC analysts,” he answered slowly.

She locked eyes with him. “The geniuses who figured him for a terrorist? The ones who convinced Morgan to leak Wheaton’s name on the internet? How do you think the Heritage Brotherhood found him, Connelly? Your precious NCTC led them right to his front door. There’s no chance I’m giving these papers to the NCTC.” Her gaze hardened. “Or you, for that matter.”

“Sasha, don’t do this. Those papers could have national security implications. I’m going to have to—”

A massive crash, like a table being overturned, or chairs being thrown, sounded from the break room just outside the door. A furious shout rose, "Chase, you son of a bitch!"

He put a hand on his holster and called up a mental image of the building. The closest exit was the blind metal door that he'd parked near that first day. It was just through the break room and then down a short hallway that doglegged to the right.

"Who's Chase?" she whispered.

"I am."

"You killed Essiah! Get out here, so I can kick your ass." The words were a guttural scream.

"Listen, there's a back exit. You just need to go through the break room and head to the right. Get out of here."

"What about you?"

"They're drunk, and they're civilians. I might have to fight a few of them, but it'll be fine."

"Don't shoot anybody unless you have no other choice."

"Thanks for the vote of confidence."

She whirled around and grabbed his collar. She pressed her face into his neck. "I'm still mad at you. But don't get hurt."

He kissed the crown of her head. "I'm not going to

get hurt. I love you. I'll call you when I get out of here and we can figure out next steps. Let Hank know what's happening if you can. I don't understand where these guys got the idea that I killed Wheaton."

She nodded into his shirt. Then she gave a quiet gasp and raised her eyes to his.

"The guys. I was about to tell you and then Dana came in. Two men were watching the building when I got here. They came in not long after me, looking for somebody. They're both wearing cowboy boots, jeans, and those big old belt buckles."

"Like they do in Texas?"

"Exactly."

He reconsidered his plan. If Holden's men had fingered him, they'd no doubt shown Wheaton's buddies copies of the pictures. Maybe he was going to have to shoot his way out.

This was not good. And then it got worse.

"Sirens," Sasha said with a tremor in her voice.

"They're still a ways off."

She glanced at the waitress, still prone on the floor. Her eyes darted from side to side and she pressed her lips together in a firm line. She was calculating a plan. After a moment, she nodded.

"No offense, but your plan sucks. Follow my lead."

"What's the play?"

"No time. Just trust me. But you're going out the back door. I'm walking out the front with my new friend."

She shouldered her bag and crouched beside the waitress.

Outside, the shouts were getting angrier.

"Dana? Dana, wake up." She gave her a little shake.

"What?" Dana struggled to a seated position and looked around, bleary-eyed, trying to get her bearings.

Sasha helped her to her feet. "Come on. We need to get you home so you can rest."

Dana nodded and got to her feet unsteadily. Sasha put an arm around the taller woman's waist, and Dana looped her arm around Sasha's shoulder.

She turned to Leo. "Ready."

He shook out his hands. "Let's do it."

Sasha opened the door and stepped out into the break room, still supporting Dana.

He followed the two women.

C.J. and Slim stood in the middle of the room, feet planted wide, fists up. Ready to fight. Closer to the door, the two cowboys Sasha had described stood off to the side. One of them had a bottle of beer in his right hand. They both had short buzzed hair, tanned faces, and massive forearms. The metal table lay on its side near the wall on the left side of the room.

Leo stepped around Sasha and raised his hands in

an appeasing gesture. "Let's take it easy, fellas."

Slim growled. "It's a little late to talk your way out of this. They saw you creeping around Essiah's place." He jerked a thumb toward the pair near the door. "Bill already called the cops. You're trapped."

It was a fair assessment.

Sasha cleared her throat. "Is one of you named C.J.?"

C.J. gave her a boozy, uncertain nod. "I am."

"Your girlfriend's not feeling well. Maybe you want to call her a cab?"

C.J. shot Slim a worried look then turned his attention back to his girlfriend. "You okay, baby?"

Dana groaned. "I think I'm gonna be sick."

Slim's nostrils flared. "Get her out of here," he told C.J.

"I can help you," Sasha offered. "We should get to the bathroom."

C.J. dropped his fists. "Thanks. Come on, baby." He walked around to Dana's other side and hugged her to his side. "I got her. You get the door."

Sasha crossed the room, skirting Holden's men, and pulled the door open. As C.J. and Dana shuffled through it, she pierced Leo with a stare. He watched the rise and fall of her throat as she swallowed. Then she tightened her grip on her bag and followed them out into the hallway.

35

Sasha kept one hand wrapped around the thick straps and hugged the bag to her body as she followed Dana and C.J. to the ladies room. The rest of the crowd at the bar appeared to be oblivious to the scene happening in the break room.

That was good. But it wouldn't last long. The sirens were growing louder.

They reached the bathroom.

"Do you want me to go in with you?" she asked Dana.

The boyfriend threw her a grateful look.

Dana shook her head. "No, I'll be okay." She pushed through the door and disappeared inside.

"I didn't think she had that much to drink," C.J. mumbled.

"She didn't. But it just hit her hard—no sleep, no food, and I'm sure emotions have been high around here since ... you know."

He nodded. "Is that guy really your husband?"

"Yeah. But he didn't kill your friend."

"I know what I saw, lady." Anger flared in his eyes.

"He's a federal agent. Essiah got himself mixed up in something he shouldn't have. I don't think he did anything wrong, but he got on the wrong side of some very bad people. My husband was trying to help him, not hurt him."

She wasn't actually sure what Connelly had been trying to do, but there was no reason to bare her soul to this guy.

He narrowed his eyes. "Then who killed him?"

"I don't know for sure, but my money's on your new friends with the cowboy boots."

His jaw hinged and his mouth fell open. "We gotta tell somebody! The police are on their way. C'mon." He started back toward the break room.

She put a hand on his arm to stop him. "He can take care of himself. You take care of Dana. And don't drive anywhere. Can you call someone for a ride?"

He nodded slowly, but his eyes kept going to the break room door. "Yeah. But, are you sure about this?"

No. Not even remotely.

"Yes," she said. "I'm sure. Listen, I'm going to go now. Make sure Dana gets something into her stomach. Maybe some crackers."

"Uh ... okay." He bobbled his head, slightly dazed by the latest turn of events.

She gave him a reassuring smile and speed-walked through the bar's main room. Her heart pounded and her leg muscles twitched, desperate to obey the signal her brain was sending them: *Run. Run!*

No, she told herself firmly. *Stay cool.* She pulled back her shoulders and kept walking.

As she was pushing open the door to the parking lot, she ran smack into two uniformed police officers on their way in.

"Officers," she said in greeting.

"Ma'am." The male officer nodded.

His partner gave a distracted look at the Battleship game she carried on her hip, but held the door open for her.

"Thanks."

The female officer holding the door didn't respond. She was busy arguing with her partner.

"C'mon, Lewis. I don't want to get twisted up because we didn't wait for the feds. They'll be here in a minute. Just stand down until they get here."

He rounded on her. "Why are we letting a bunch of

dweebs from the FBI take over, Macklyn? This is our murder, in our jurisdiction."

Sasha'd heard enough. She raced toward her car.

The FBI was on its way. That was good for Connelly. Wasn't it? At this point, she wasn't sure. Usually, he and Hank worked independent of the official channels. Would the FBI even know about his assignment, whatever it was?

The growing sensation that her husband was a virtual stranger threatened to overwhelm her. It was a distraction she didn't have time for right now.

She rested her bag in the foot well of the passenger seat, placed the box beside it, jammed the key into the ignition, and started the car. She zipped out of the parking lot and headed for the highway.

Before she had the chance to call Hank, her phone rang. She activated the hands-free feature.

"This is Sasha."

"It's Naya. Your friend Angela Washington called again."

"I left her a voicemail and told her Gella's not available this morning, what's her deal?" She didn't have time for this.

"I've got her on hold. I'll conference her in because you're never gonna believe this. She's bargaining against herself."

Sasha heard two short beeps then Naya was back.

"Attorney Washington?"

"Here."

"Sasha?"

"Yep."

"Excellent. So, Ms. Washington, why don't you repeat your client's new offer for Sasha's benefit."

"Hi, Sasha. I know your decision maker is out of pocket, but I have a new offer for you to communicate. She can take the weekend to think about this one. I have to imagine it'll be a fairly easy decision, though. I was just telling your partner that my clients have jointly decided they really want to head off a long and distracting legal battle that could drag on for years. They're willing to increase their offer to seven hundred and fifty thousand dollars in exchange for a dismissal with prejudice of the complaint and your client's signature on a non-disclosure agreement."

"I need to be sure I understand. You're offering three-quarters of a million dollars, pre-discovery, pre-briefing to make this case go away?"

"Yes, I'd say that's quite generous. Wouldn't you?" Angela Washington sounded inordinately pleased with herself; her tone was just this side of gloating.

"Actually, I'd say that's desperate."

"I beg your pardon?"

"Your clients must be worried that something pretty damaging could come to light to make this offer."

"That's absurd."

"Is it? So Sentinel Solution Systems isn't concerned that their actions may have resulted in a murder?"

"I have no idea what you're talking about."

"Right. And let me guess, this dismissal would be drafted in such a way as to prevent my client from bringing suit against anyone else on these grounds, wouldn't it?"

"Well, yes. But there's no other entity you could sue for the alleged data leak, anyway."

"Sure there is. Listen, Angela, I'm in the car and I can't really talk. Put your offer in writing. I'll forward it to my client with my recommendation. In the meantime, I'll continue to research my client's possible claims against the National Counterterrorism Center. I'll be in touch when DoGiveThrive's made a decision."

"You can't sue the NCTC."

"Sure I can."

The woman sputtered. Naya muffled a laugh.

"I have to end the call now. Goodbye, Angela. I'll talk to you later, Naya."

She disconnected the call. She would have loved to call Naya back and dissect the bizarre offer in detail, but she had other priorities at the moment.

"Call Hank," she said.

Hank answered right away. "Richardson."

"I found Connelly. He's at a bar in Mars. The place is called Mugsy's, and he's got himself in a jam."

"What kind of jam? Are you there now?"

"I'm in my car. I left, but he's still there. Two guys, who we're pretty sure are working for the Heritage Brotherhood, have convinced some bikers that Connelly killed Mr. Wheaton. He's outnumbered and the police are there, but they're currently standing in the doorway arguing over whether to call the FBI."

"He told you about the Heritage Brotherhood?" Hank sounded furious.

"No. We found some of Essiah's papers."

"Good. And don't worry about the police. I spoke to Leo after you and I last talked. Our boss is going to make the connection between Leo and Mr. Wheaton go away."

"What do you mean, make it go away?"

"I don't know the substance of her conversations, and I wouldn't share them if I did. But she spoke to Washington and has received assurances that the matter's being cleaned up."

Sasha's surreal conversation with Angela Washington was still top of mind. If it hadn't been, the statement would have slipped right past her.

"When you say she spoke to Washington, do you

mean someone in Washington? Or someone named Washington?"

He chuckled. "Both, actually. There's a talented young attorney working on some matters for this task force we're on."

Sasha clenched the steering wheel. "Her name wouldn't happen to be Angela Washington, would it?"

"As a matter of fact, it would. You know her?"

"You could say that. She's trying her hardest to make sure the NCTC doesn't get caught up in a lawsuit. You guys think you can buy your way out of taking responsibility for what you've done." Her hands shook, but her voice was steady. "I can't believe this."

"I don't know what anyone else has done or not done, but every action Leo took was authorized and appropriate, Sasha."

She barely heard him through the haze of anger clouding her mind.

He rambled on. "And the papers you two found will probably go a long way toward explaining what happened to Essiah Wheaton and toward making the country a safer place."

"Not really. They're written in code."

"Doesn't matter. Leo can just turn them over to the—"

"No, he can't. He doesn't have them. I do."

"I'll meet you somewhere so you can hand them off. Where are you now?"

Sasha stared through the windshield at the highway unfolding in front of her car. She felt a spark of fire in her chest. She sat up straighter.

"No."

"What do you mean, no? You can't be running around with sensitive information that might jeopardize ongoing national security activities."

"Watch me."

He lowered his voice a notch and spoke in a dangerous whisper. "This isn't a game. And if you think you can play on our friendship and your relationship with Leo to jerk me around and get away with it, you're sadly mistaken."

She signaled to move to the left lane and passed a line of slower moving cars. After she swung the car back into the right travel lane, she took a deep breath and said what she had to say.

"I know it's not a game. A man is dead. But you guys started this with your stupid NCTC information request. And now this lawyer of yours is throwing money at me and my client to keep us quiet. I don't think so. I don't trust you not to mishandle these papers. And when I say you, I mean any of you, including my husband."

Just hearing the words come out of her mouth made

her wince, but they were true. Connelly had never made a secret of his unwavering loyalty to the government. To him, loyalty to country and loyalty to his department head were one and the same.

"You can't just refuse to turn them over."

"Actually, I can. Want to know why?"

"I'd love to."

"Because I also have the envelope with the letter claiming Connelly killed Mr. Wheaton *and* I have the pictures that place him on the property less than twenty-four hours before the man was strangled. If you or anybody else tries to interfere with me in any way, then I'll give the pictures to Maisy and tell her to air a story naming Connelly, you, and your boss as members of a secret government agency that killed an American citizen."

He was silent for a moment. "Are you out of your mind?"

"Maybe I am, Hank. But he's keeping secrets, and I don't know if I can trust you. So we're going to do this my way."

When he spoke again, she heard him gritting his teeth. "You're playing with fire, Sasha. If I don't have those papers in my hand by the end of the day, there's gonna be hell to pay."

She checked the time. It was twelve-thirty. She'd be

home by one. Plenty of time to decode the papers and figure out her next steps. She hoped.

“I can work with that.”

“Oh, I’m so pleased that meets with your approval.”

He ended the call with an angry click.

That was the thing about mobile phones, she mused. There were no satisfying hang ups, anymore. The art of slamming the phone down in someone’s ear had vanished.

36

Leo waited until Sasha had cleared out of the room with CJ and his girlfriend. He suppressed a smile. Leave it to her to get rid of one of his adversaries. Now it was only three against one—close enough to a fair fight that he thought the odds were good he wouldn't need to pull his gun.

His primary concern wasn't Slim. But if the guys in the boots actually were members of the Heritage Brotherhood, they might have some paramilitary training. The tall one didn't look overly menacing. But he didn't like the way the short, stockier guy was hanging onto that beer bottle. All he'd have to do was smash the neck and he'd have a handy, deadly weapon.

Don't get ahead of yourself. That's how people end up trigger-happy.

He turned his attention back to Slim but kept the other two in his peripheral vision.

"Slim, I know there are pictures floating around that show me on Essiah's property."

Slim glanced over his left shoulder at the men standing along the wall. "How do you explain that?"

"I wasn't there to kill him. And my name's not really Chase." He reached for his leather holder and flipped it open one-handed to reveal his old marshal badge. "My name is Leo Connelly. I'm a federal agent, and these two men are implicated in an investigation I'm not at liberty to discuss."

Slim's eyes widened. The other two men didn't react.

"Is this for real?"

"Yes. Now, I want to you to turn around and leave. Clear the area around the door and have Bill send the police straight back here when they get here, okay?"

"Uh, sure." Slim spared one final look at the two guys before he scurried out of the room.

"Well," Leo said, "you two sure are quiet."

The taller of the two glanced at the one with the beer bottle. As Leo had anticipated, the stocky guy was in charge.

"You're not much of an agent. We could've picked you off the other night and you never would've seen it coming," the boss drawled. Then he took a pull of his beer.

Leo ignored the dig. Letting an opponent get inside your head with trash talk was strictly for amateurs.

"What's your name?" he pointed his chin at the tall guy.

"Uh, Marcus."

"Are you freaking kidding me? Don't answer his questions." His tanned face reddened and he gripped the bottle tighter.

"Sorry, Chuck." The name flew from the man's mouth before he thought it through. When he realized what he'd said he clamped his hand over his mouth.

Leo did grin this time as he amended his odds. It was more like one against one, after all.

Chuck tossed back the last swallow of beer and hit the bottle against the wall in one smooth motion. The glass shattered, leaving him holding the mouth of the bottle and a jagged collar below.

Leo pressed his lips in a firm line and drew his weapon.

"Don't move."

The man ignored his instruction. Instead, he snaked out his free arm and grabbed Marcus. He pulled him close and pressed the bottle against his exposed neck.

"Ch-Chuck?" Marcus managed.

"Yeah, really. What kind of brotherhood are you guys in?"

Marcus's eyes got big at the mention of the brotherhood. Chuck pushed the edge of the broken bottle harder into his neck. Marcus sucked in a breath. He flinched as several bright red droplets of blood bubbled up.

"Hey, take it easy," Leo said.

He hadn't bargained for one of the guys being a psychopath.

"I need to clean up some loose ends," Chuck snarled.

Marcus stiffened.

So much for that plan not to fire his weapon. But he wasn't just going to stand here and watch this guy slit his buddy's throat open with a piece of glass. Even if his buddy was a piece of crap.

He locked eyes with Marcus.

"You don't know me, so let me tell you a few things. Protocol is for me to negotiate with you, convince you that it's in your best interest to let this guy go. Or at least stall you until a sharpshooter can get into position and take a kill shot. But here's the thing, I don't really care if you kill your friend. If you pieces of trash start killing each other, it's really just less clean-up work for us, you know?"

Marcus stared at him bug-eyed.

He went on. "But bleeding out from a neck wound seems like an unnecessarily painful way to go. So, I'd like to shoot him you know? A head shot, boom. It's over before Marcus knows what happening."

Leo paused here for effect.

He glanced at Marcus and noticed the dark wet stain spreading across the crotch of his jeans. *Dude.*

"Now, Marcus would probably rather I shoot *you* in the head. Odds are you'd be dead before you could slash that bottle across his neck, but even if your dying act is to kill him, that's really no skin off my nose."

They were both gaping at him now. He just had to keep the emotionless killer character going a while longer.

"But then there's all that paperwork. That probably sounds cruel, but we're talking about a lot of forms. So, in summary, these solutions don't appeal to me. What are your thoughts, Chuck? Think quick, though. The police'll be here any minute."

Chuck lowered the piece of glass and pushed Marcus away. Leo kept the gun trained on him.

"You're crazy," Chuck informed him.

Leo shrugged. Marcus huddled on the floor, sobbing.

"Takes one to know one, I guess. At least I didn't piss myself." He jerked his head toward the guy on the floor.

Chuck followed his eyes and let out a disgusted sigh.

"So, now what?" Leo said.

Chuck whaled the chunk of glass at his head like a fastball. He ducked and it smashed into the wall behind him. By the time he straightened to standing, Chuck was out the door, running down the hall to the back exit.

He cursed and holstered the gun as he ran after the man. Slim was standing in the doorway to the main barroom, his chest puffed out and his arms crossed, keeping everyone out of the area like he'd been told to do. Good man.

Leo skidded to a stop beside him. "The tall guy's back there, crying. His buddy turned on him. Get a couple guys to grab him and hold him until the police get here. He either killed Essiah or knows who did."

Slim nodded and gestured for two of his friends to join him. Leo took off down the hall and exploded through the door to the parking lot.

Chuck was trucking across the lot, running toward a blue Toyota. Leo turned on the speed and ran him down.

He tackled the shorter man around the waist and pulled him to the asphalt. He was about to drive a knee into his back to keep him there when he bucked and flipped over.

Leo got a fistful of his shirt and pulled back his right fist. He connected square with brittle cheekbone, and the man's head bobbled to the side. He followed up with a sharp left jab and caught him in the nose.

Chuck wiped blood and snot from his face, reared his head back and lunged forward.

Head-butt incoming, Leo thought. He ducked and juked to the side.

Chuck grinned wolfishly and clamped his teeth over Leo's left ear.

He yelped in pain as the man bit down hard. Blood trickled down the side of his neck. The bastard still had his ear between his teeth. He was going to bite it clean off.

Leo scrabbled for his gun. He got a hold of it and jammed it into Chuck's chest. Chuck relaxed his jaw, and Leo jerked his head back to get his ear out of the man's mouth.

Just then, he felt cold metal pressed against the back of his skull.

"Drop it, nice and easy, then put your hands up." The female voice spoke loudly and clearly.

"I'm with the Department of Homeland Security. Agent Leo Connelly," he told her.

“That’s nice. I’m Officer Kristin Macklyn.”

“This is an active investigation.”

“Great. We can sort it out when your pals from the FBI get here. Seems they got turned around. Again. Your boys need to get some better navigation systems … or learn to read maps.” She toed him in the back with a dress shoe. “Drop the weapon.”

“This man’s wanted in connection with the murder of Essiah Wheaton, officer,” he tried again.

“Don’t worry, he’s not going anywhere, either. I’m not going to tell you again.”

Leo huffed out an irritated breath and tossed his gun on the pavement and raised his hands.

“I’m going to need to call my boss.”

37

Fletch pressed the phone to his ear to listen to Marcus's babbling as he moved around his basement office, quickly but calmly putting his plans into motion.

As soon as Marcus had spit out the words "federal agent, police, and Chuck's in custody," Fletch had opened his combination safe and removed a Smith and Wesson, a stack of bills, and his passport. One good thing about porous borders was that he'd be in Mexico before Chuck was done being processed.

He did have to hand it to Marcus. Who'd have thought the guy would've had the stones to run for it.

"So you said you needed to use the facilities, and these idiots just let you go in by yourself?" He shook his head in amazement.

"Yes, sir. Well, I'd had ... an accident. They thought that was hilarious, so they made me use the ladies' room. And, of course, none of them wanted to go in there."

An accident? He decided he didn't want to know any details.

"And you climbed out a window and got clean away, huh?"

"I did. So ... what should I do now?"

Fletcher didn't give a good goshdarn what this fool did now.

"Keep your head down and get your ass back home, I reckon."

"About the files, I mean."

"The files?"

"I hid inside a dumpster until the police left with Agent Connelly and Chuck."

This effing guy. First he pees himself, then he hides in a dumpster.

"So?"

"Agent Connelly made two phone calls. He walked away from the crowd to talk privately. He was standing maybe ten feet from me. I heard every word he said."

"And he said something about Wheaton's files?"

"He called his boss first. Apparently, Essiah hid the

files in a locker at the bar. This Agent Connelly, his wife had been there earlier—"

"It's take your wife to work day at the FBI? What?"

"I don't think he's FBI. Maybe Homeland Security? I'm not sure. But this wife of his—I saw her, she's an itty-bitty thing. You could fit her in your pocket. She took the files with her. His boss sounded hopping mad about it."

"Yeah. I'll bet."

"Then he called the wife. It sounded like Wheaton must've used a code or something because he asked her if she'd had any luck cracking it. Then he told her to keep at it. He said he'd be a couple hours because he had to give a statement about Chuck and all to the local police."

Chuck. It was a crying shame that his most useful lieutenant had gone and gotten himself arrested.

"So, what are you saying, Marcus? Are you telling me you think you're up for getting those files off this woman?"

Marcus bristled. "I know I am."

"And you say she's tiny?"

"She can't weigh a hundred pounds and she probably needs a booster seat to drive."

Fletch chuckled. "I would like to have those files back."

Marcus blurted, “And I’d like a shot at filling the spot Chuck’s absence will leave vacant, sir.”

“Well, I’ll be. You’ve got more fire in your belly than I gave you credit for, son.”

“Thank you. I’ll be honest, though. I do have a personal interest in getting my hands on those papers. I was one of the original straw man investors, if you recall.”

“I do.” Yessir, Marcus’s name would be all over the fake loans they’d taken out using Essiah Wheaton’s banker’s license. There were more than a handful of men who had good reason to want those files.

“I’ll tell you what, Marcus. Let’s consider this a job interview. You get those documents, and the security post is yours.”

“Yes, sir. I do have a question.”

“Shoot.”

“That’s the question. Am I authorized to kill her?”

“Mrs. Connelly, you mean?”

“Yes.”

“I’m not authorizing you—I’m *ordering* you. If there’s any chance she broke that code and read those papers, she’s got to die. Are we clear?”

“Crystal.”

“Wait, don’t you need me to get you her address or something?”

"My son's taken care of that. He can hack just about any system you can imagine." Marcus's voice swelled with pride.

"Well, what are you waiting for then? Saddle up and ride."

Fletch ended the call and rubbed his nose. Maybe he didn't have to head down to Mexico just yet, after all. He surely didn't want to leave Melody Lynn alone up here where she might get bored and get into trouble. He tossed the stack of bills back into the safe then placed the passport and gun on top of the cash.

Marcus Seton. He never would've thunk it. He slapped his thigh and laughed.

Shoot, since it looked like his day was turning around, maybe he oughta go play some cards. He reached into the safe and took out the money.

38

Sasha checked the time. Four p.m. It had been almost three hours since Connelly had called to tell her the men who killed Essiah Wheaton had been taken into custody. And then called back to tell her one of them had escaped.

As far as she was concerned, she was glad one of them had gotten away. Because if Connelly and Hank were busy with a manhunt, she might have more time to figure out Wheaton's code. Her parents were going to take the kids to their favorite Mexican restaurant for dinner, so she had a couple more hours to wrestle with it.

What was she missing?

She picked up the copies she'd made on the compact home copier/printer/scanner that she and

Connelly shared and studied the first page again. Line after line of numbers broken into series of varying lengths with no apparent pattern. The numbers were all one- and two-digit values—the largest number was ten, and the most common number, by far, was one. Each number in a set was separated by a hyphen.

He'd been a banker. Maybe these were just bank account numbers.

Eighteen pages filled with nothing but bank accounts? That hardly seemed useful. She had to be missing something. Something obvious. One through ten. What did it mean?

At first, she'd figured the key had to be related to Battleship. Even though the horizontal axis on the game grid only went to nine, and the vertical axis was lettered A through H, she figured Wheaton had created a substitution code, using numerals. But she'd wasted hours messing around with the grid and nothing she'd tried worked.

Time was running out.

Maybe the numbers were page and line numbers in a common book. Maybe the dictionary. It was a long shot. But, at this point, she'd try anything.

She crossed to the room to the bookshelf, stretched up on her toes, and grabbed the thick dictionary they used to settle challenges during Scrabble matches from its spot on top of the bookcase. They stored it next to the Scrabble game because it was too large to shelve. As she pulled the heavy book down, it bumped against the Scrabble box, which tumbled off the shelf and hit the ground. Tiles scattered across the floor.

She crouched to gather them up. As she was dropping a Q into the tile bag, she noted the value. Ten points for a Q. The only other ten-point letter was Z, which made 'quiz' a no-brainer and Connelly's go-to word.

She stared down at the letters fanned out on her floor.

It couldn't be that easy.

Could it?

An image of her hands lifting a well-used Scrabble box out of Essiah's locker flashed in her mind.

Her pulse fluttered.

She shoved the rest of the tiles into the bag and flipped the playing board open to study the tile distribution and value chart printed along the left side of the board. She grabbed a pen and the top sheet from her stack of copies and examined the rows of numbers.

She shifted her attention to the chart then back to the numbers. And then she tossed her pen on the desk in disgust. There were too many possible letters that '1' could represent. If he'd used his Scrabble tiles, she'd *never* figure it out.

She stared harder at the sheet.

He hadn't just used the tiles. He'd used the board layout, too. Series of figures branched off from one another vertically and horizontally, but never diagonally.

If she could just determine a handful of the keystone words, she'd probably be able to figure out the ones that branched off them, too. There was only one 'K' tile, worth five points. She'd start there.

Of course, there weren't any Ks on the first sheet. She flipped through the pages and wrote a 'K' in place of every '5.' Her brain buzzed. This was almost as satisfying as finding the perfect case to fit a client's fact pattern.

Assuming it works, she cautioned herself.

Back to the chart. Now for the ten-pointers. She dug through Connelly's pencil cup until she found one with both a point and an eraser. She wrote a 'Q/Z' for every instance of a '10.'

It was going to get trickier as the more common values came into play. There were ten possible letters that a '1' could represent. But, she reasoned, five of those were vowels, and she'd be able to tell by their position within words whether some of them were vowels or consonants. Her Sunday morning crossword puzzle habit was about to pay dividends.

She spread out the papers and got to work.

When she looked up, the sun had dipped out of view and the clock over the desk showed it was nearly seven o'clock. She reached for her phone and thumbed out a text to her mother:

Can kids spend the night? Deadline. I'll owe you.

The response came through instantly:

Don't be silly. We'd love to keep them. I have pjs in the spare room from last time.

She exhaled:

Thanks.

Another text came through:

Finn says he hasn't seen daddy in weeks. That's not true, is it?

She shook her head:

No. He's not the most reliable timekeeper, Mom. Everything's fine here. We just both have time-sensitive things for work and L had to travel this week. Thanks for helping with the kids. XOXOXO

She discarded the phone and looked down at her progress so far:

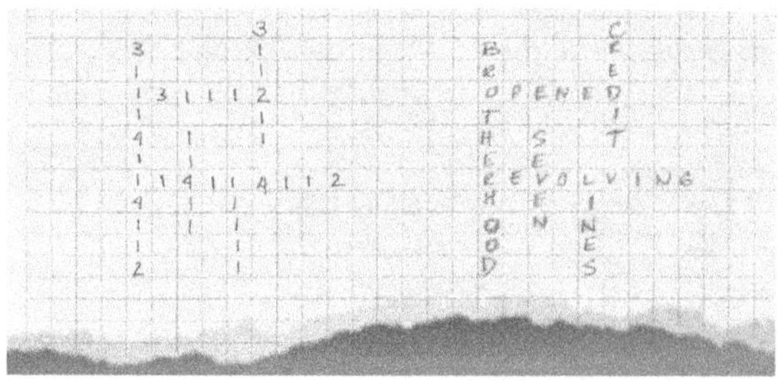

She laughed out loud. She did it. She cracked the code.

She reached for her phone again. Should she call Connelly first? Or Hank? She hesitated.

She owed it to Essiah Wheaton to figure out everything he knew. After all, he'd been murdered because of his knowledge. What if Leo and Hank turned the papers over to the NCTC or the FBI or whoever, and they decided not to pursue anything? Essiah would've died in vain.

You have the copies, remember? Just give them the origi-

nals and keep working. You don't even have to tell them you figured it out.

That last part would never fly, she knew. Connelly would take one look at her face and know. She rubbed at a tight knot in her neck and tried to decide what to do next. Her phone's battery blinked red and then shut down, drained.

Well that settles that, she thought. She wouldn't be calling anyone until she charged her phone. She found Connelly's charger in the tangle of wires and cords on the desk, plugged in the dead device, and returned to the code.

Within minutes, a motive for murder had appeared on the page:

```
BROTHERHOOD OPENED SEVEN REVOLVING
CREDIT LINES WITH BOGUS DOCUMENTS
USED THEM TO LAUNDER MONEY FROM
ARMS SALES
CHUCK ACCESSED BANK LINK FROM MY
MACHINE
LOANS GENERATED UNDER MY ID
QUESTIONED FLH ABOUT ACTIVITY
TOLD TO ZIP MY MOUTH IF I WANTED
TO LIVE
```

Below the window, two of the bright motion-sensing lights bloomed to life in the backyard. Mocha started barking and raced up the stairs from the kitchen. Java, who was sleeping atop the printer, opened one eye at the racket.

Mocha skidded to a stop at her feet and whined.

"What's the matter, boy? Did a squirrel set off the lights again? You're gonna get that squirrel someday, yes you are."

She scratched behind his ears. He was never going to get close to that squirrel. But everybody needed to have a dream.

From downstairs, the sound of shattering glass echoed through the house.

She froze and tried to listen over the sound of blood rushing in her ears.

The crashing noise had come from the kitchen. The window over the sink, maybe.

Mocha bared his teeth. She pulled her hand back. He never growled. But that was a definite growl rumbling in his chest.

He seemed to shrink, making himself low to the ground. His ears were flattened over his head. He crept under the desk, covered his nose with his paws, and whimpered.

Java got to his feet, puffed himself out like a

furball, and jumped lightly to the floor. He ran under the desk and wedged himself in the corner behind the dog.

Gooseflesh rose on her arms. Her heart thumped.

"Okay, you two are freaking me out."

The house was too still. And her animals knew. Something was wrong.

She grabbed the stack of papers she'd been working on. Nearly running, she wheeled the desk chair to the closet. She pulled the gun safe down to the floor and crouched in front of it.

She slammed her index finger on the fingerprint reader and waited, jittering her leg.

The light flashed, the beep sounded, and the spring-loaded door opened. Her breathing was fast, shallow. She did not need to be operating with insufficient oxygen right now. She forced herself to take deep, slow breaths.

She heard the creak of the loose floorboard on the eighth step from the top of the stairs.

Someone was coming.

She exhaled then reached inside for the Sig Sauer. She felt nothing but air?

Not possible.

She peered inside. Empty.

Her heart thudded and her mind spun dizzily. This

wasn't possible. It had been here the night before last. She'd held it in her hands.

The laundry.

Connelly had been home. Why he needed two handguns, she had no idea. What she *did* know was there was an intruder in her home. She was unarmed. The only phone on the premises had a dead battery. And she was holding a stack of papers the Heritage Brotherhood was willing to kill for.

She didn't like her odds.

She shoved the copies inside the safe then closed and locked it. She stood up and pulled the closet doors closed without a sound.

She sidled along the wall until she reached the doorway, then she yanked the door shut and locked it from the inside.

Avoid the conflict.

She'd caught a glimpse of the man's startled face just before she slammed the door closed. She recognized him. He was the taller of the two guys from the bar—the one who'd escaped from the police. And he had a gun. It dangled loosely from his right hand.

He yelled through the door. "I want Wheaton's papers." Venom laced his words.

"Okay, sure. But I'll tell you right now, they're written in code. I can't make heads or tails of it." She walked to the desk and grabbed the originals. She bumped the bottoms of the pages against the desk to square the edges then she walked back to the closed door.

She lay on her stomach. "I'm slipping them under the door. There are almost twenty pages. So, I'll do two sets, okay?"

"Just open the door."

"I don't think so."

She slid the first half of the pages under the door and peered through the crack until she saw him bend to pick them up. He gathered them and stood up.

"These are just rows of numbers."

"Like I said, I don't know what it's supposed to mean. Maybe you'll have better luck than I did. Here come the rest." She pushed them under the door.

This time he lay down out in the hallway and stared under the crack at her. She saw one brown eye and part of his eyebrow.

"How do I know that's everything?"

"I guess you're going to have to take my word for it."

"That's not good enough!" He was yelling.

"Listen, do you really think I'm going to let you come in here so you can shoot me? Really?"

"I just want to talk to you."

"So, talk. I can hear you, but I'm not opening the door."

He stood up and pounded his fist against the door.

Under the desk, Mocha started to cry.

"What's that noise?"

"Mocha, my dog. He's hiding under the desk. So's the cat. I gave you the papers. Leave."

He hammered at the door, harder. The wood was vibrating. She figured it was a matter of time before he broke the thing down.

He obviously didn't intend to let her live. She'd given him what he wanted. The only reason he would want access to her now was to kill her. And she wasn't just going to sit in here all night and wait for him to do it.

Avoidance hadn't worked. Neither had de-escalation. Her next tactic would be to escape.

She crept over to the charger and checked her phone. The battery was at one percent. Not enough juice to call Connelly or Hank.

She glanced at the closet, cursing her luck. She couldn't believe Connelly'd taken the gun; not after all the times he'd practically begged her to learn to shoot so she could defend herself.

Of course, the gun wouldn't have done her much good. She didn't know how to use it. She *did*, however, know how take down an armed assailant. But she hoped it wouldn't come to that.

Sasha tiptoed to the door on the east wall, which led to a shared Jack and Jill bathroom. The bathroom had a second door that opened into a guest bedroom she used for practicing yoga and storing mountains of client files.

She slipped out of the bathroom and slunk through the darkened room. She pressed herself against the wall and peeked out into the hall.

The guy was stretched out on the floor, still looking under the door. But as she watched, he pulled himself to his feet and turned sideways, getting ready to ram his shoulder into the door.

He was tall, taller than Connelly even, but he was thin. Unless he was much stronger than he looked, it would take him several tries to splinter the door. She might as well let him tire himself out for a bit.

He reared back and ran toward the door. She heard the impact, but the door held. For now.

He did it again. Both times, he led with his left shoulder and kept the gun in his right, aiming for the center of the door.

Now, he stopped, rubbed his shoulder, and switched the gun to his left hand. He pivoted and drove his right shoulder into the door. The wood cracked loudly as it broke apart.

Using the noise as cover, she raced out of the guest bedroom and clattered down the stairs. He shouted and came barreling down the steps behind her.

She tore through the living room to the front door, scanning the room for something, *anything*, to use as a weapon. Nothing remotely promising caught her eye.

Too late, she felt something under her foot and looked down in time to watch herself slip on a blue cylindrical wooden block from the twins building set. Her ankle rolled to the side and she yelped.

She tried to regain her balance but she was moving too quickly to recalibrate. She flew up and over the block structure then landed with a thud on her side. Colorful blocks scattered across the floor.

She clambered to her knees.

Her assailant caught up to her and grabbed a chunk of her hair, wrapped it around his left fist, and yanked back on her head with enough force to make her eyes water. The barrel of the gun pressed into the back of her head.

This was a very bad position to be in. On her knees, with no leverage, and a gun she could neither see nor reach pointed at the back of her head, execution-style.

She closed her eyes and willed herself to stay calm. The victor in this battle would be whoever managed to stay in control. She gathered her thoughts, opened her eyes, and twisted her head to see him. Her scalp protested the motion; it felt as if her hair were being ripped out by the roots.

She panted. “I lied to you. I did figure out the code.”

She watched for the moment when he started to process her words. His eyes flitted briefly away from hers while he tried to decide if she was telling the truth.

“You’re lying.”

“I’m not. Just let go of my hair so I can think and I’ll tell you.”

“Turn back around. Keep your eyes forward.”

She did as he said. He released his grip on her hair but pushed the gun into her skull as a warning.

“Start talking.”

“He was a Scrabble player. Do you play?”

“What?”

“Do you understand the point values of the letter tiles?”

She waited for him to answer. Daniel had pounded the principle into her skull, and her experience confirmed it: The best time to disarm someone is when they’re distracted.

“Sure,” he said. “The more common the letter is the fewer points it’s worth, but the—”

She shifted her body weight to the left, out of the line of fire, and turned slightly while she shot her right hand up and clamped it down over the top of the barrel of the gun.

He yanked back on the weapon.

With her dominant left hand, she grabbed the inside of his right wrist and immobilized his right forearm.

He swung his left fist around and punched her in the side of the head. Her face vibrated from the strike.

She pulled his right arm forward over her shoulder, pushed his hand and the gun to the right, and twisted them both sideways, gaining control of the gun's trajectory. She planted her feet under her and pushed her body weight back so that her shoulder drove into his locked elbow.

Then she pushed down on his wrist and slammed it against the floor while yanking on the gun with her other hand. He cursed, red-faced with pain, and his grip loosened. She wrenched the weapon free and sent it skittering across the room.

She pulled him forward while she flipped onto her back.

She was basically under him now—a terrible position that would have made Daniel foam at the mouth. But she still controlled his dominant hand. So, all in all, it wasn't the worst ground fight she'd experienced.

He punched at her with his left hand. She rolled her head to the side and the blow glanced off.

Wishing she weren't barefoot, she aimed a flurry of kicks directly between his legs with her right leg. He grunted and lurched forward.

She straightened her leg and planted a rock-solid kick on the bottom of his chin. Then she extended her leg again and kicked him square in the nose.

He tore his right arm free of her grip and pinned her to the ground with his knees. He pressed his left hand down on her right shoulder, forcing her arm up over her head.

Well, she acknowledged, *this ground fight just got a lot worse.*

She groped around behind her blindly with her right hand until she reached one of the large rectangular blocks that formed the base of almost all castles and forts the kids made. She wrapped her fingers around it and clamped her fist shut.

She was only going to get one chance at this.

With her free left hand, she grabbed a fistful of his tee shirt and pulled him close, yanking his head toward her as if she were going to kiss him. At the same time she lifted her shoulders and neck from the ground, moving up to meet him.

Confusion clouded his face.

She seized the moment to rotate her right shoulder inward toward her ear and twist her shoulder free from his grasp. She swung her right arm up as if she were casting a fishing line and brought it around to the unprotected back of his head and smashed the block into the groove behind his mastoid bone, right in the small hollow where his neck muscles met his skull.

His eyes went blank from the blow to the lesser occipital nerve, and he lost consciousness instantly.

Yes.

Her celebration at knocking him out was cut short by the realization that he was pitching forward, straight toward her, like a felled tree.

Crap.

She struggled to free herself, but she was trapped. She tucked her chin and turned her head to avoid a direct hit and his massive forehead bounced off her temple before continuing its journey to the floor.

He landed with a resounding thud that sounded just a bit too thunderous to her ringing ears. She turned woozily to see Connelly, followed by Hank, crash through the front door, guns drawn.

She pushed her assailant to the side and wiped away the blood streaming down the side of her face. She staggered to her feet and turned to greet her husband, swaying slightly. Then the world went black.

39

"I'm fine," Sasha insisted weakly.

Connelly pursed his lips like a strict teacher. "Shhh."

She struggled to pull herself upright against the piles of pillows. Java protested the movement and dug her claws into Sasha's lap.

"I'm serious. It was a glancing blow."

"And I'm serious. You need to rest."

"I don't have a concussion. The EMT said it as clear as day before he left. I have a headache and some slight dizziness. That's it."

Also some nausea, blurred vision, and ringing in her ears, but he was already overreacting. No need to give him more ammunition.

"And there's no harm in staying up tonight to keep an eye on you, just in case."

She sighed.

He handed her another cup of herbal tea. "Here, drink this."

She shot him a black look but sipped the hot tisane. "I'm glad you guys got here when you did."

"Yeah, me, too. It's been a while since I've had to save your butt."

"A while? Try *ever*. Including tonight. I knocked him out, before you and Hank got here, remember? And I came to before he did. I had everything under control ... ish."

He grinned and joined her on the couch. "Scooch over. So, what should we do to pass the time until morning?" he asked, dropping his arm around her shoulder and pulling her snug against his side to the cat's extreme displeasure.

"Are you serious about staying up all night?"

"Yes."

She eyed him. "We could play Scrabble. Sorta?"

"Sorta Scrabble?"

"You know how Hank took Wheaton's papers when he left?"

"Yes."

"I might have made copies."

"You don't say. Might you also have stashed them in the gun safe?"

She looked at him wide-eyed for a moment, then she realized. "You put your guns back, didn't you?"

"I did. And I found these." He leaned forward and lifted their wedding album from the coffee table. He'd smoothed out the crumpled sheets and placed them under the heavy book in an effort to flatten them.

"If you get the scrabble board and a pen, we can finish decoding them."

"You cracked it?"

"Yep."

"No, you didn't."

She laughed at his disbelief. Then she winced. Laughing, it turned out, gave her a searing pain in her temple.

"Why didn't you tell Hank?"

"Mainly because I was unconscious."

"Okay, fair point."

She reached for his hand. "But, also, because I meant what I said. My client made a promise to Essiah Wheaton that his identity wouldn't be revealed. She broke that promise because of something the NCTC did. His blood is on *their* hands. And I want to know what was so important."

"To satisfy your curiosity?"

"Sure." She turned to face him. "And to see if his widow has grounds to sue the government."

He dropped her hand like it was a dirty diaper. "Sasha, you can't."

"Why not?"

"I *work* for the government, remember?"

"Well, *I* don't."

He exhaled through his nose. "I was ordered to kill him."

"Who? Essiah Wheaton?"

"Yes."

She gasped.

"You know I *didn't*, but that was my assignment. How long do you think it would take for that to come out if you sued the NCTC?"

A flash of heat rushed through her body, and she felt herself flush. "Are you telling me I can't do what's in my client's best interest—or Sheila Anne Johnson's?" Her voice shook with anger.

"No, I'm asking you to consider what's in my—*our*—best interest."

She stared down at her hands.

After several long moments passed in silence, he stood and cleared his throat.

"I'm going to go get the Scrabble board. You're right. We might as well work out the code."

"Fine," she said dully.

She leaned her head back against the pillows and closed her eyes.

40

Three days later

Ingrid shook her head as she read over the unredacted report. Connelly and Richardson had brought the Heritage Brotherhood to its knees. With the documents Essiah Wheaton had squirreled away, the Department of Justice had enough evidence to charge Fletcher Lee Holden with an array of felonies dating back to 2004. The names and details provided in Wheaton's cache of documents would also go a long way to shutting down a larger network of gun runners, money launderers, and assorted dirtbags.

In addition, Marcus Seton had snapped up a cooperation deal offered by the prosecutors and agreed to testify that Holden ordered the murder of Essiah

Wheaton and Chuck Price carried out the order by strangling the man. Seton was also facing charges for the attack on Connelly's wife.

Under ordinary circumstances, the resolution would be a big win for her and her team. She should be giving Richardson and Connelly commendations and kudos.

But these weren't ordinary circumstances. Complicating factors were at play. She rubbed her temple. The two men watched her without expression, waiting.

She cleared her throat. "You've done good work, there's no question."

"But?" Richardson prompted.

"But we've got a problem. Two, actually." She jabbed a finger in the air, aiming at Connelly's chest. "One, you disregarded an order."

"You're talking about the order to kill Wheaton?"

"To neutralize Wheaton."

To his credit, he didn't react to her semantic nonsense.

"Ingrid—" Hank began.

"Don't bother. I read the background. The algorithm misidentified him. He wasn't a member of the Heritage Brotherhood. They used his banking credentials without his knowledge. None of that matters. The instruction was to take care of him. You didn't."

"But the information he compiled about the

Heritage Brotherhood is what's going to bring them down. He was one of the good guys."

"It doesn't matter," she repeated.

Richardson's left eyebrow quirked up almost imperceptibly.

Connelly jutted out his jaw. "Respectfully, that's on me, ma'am. Not Agent Richardson. I disobeyed the order, not him."

"That's not how this works and you know it. He's your supervisor. It's on both of you." She picked up a slim folder from her desk and flipped it open. "I've prepared letters of censure for your files."

She studied them for a moment. Richardson's nostrils flared. A muscle in Connelly's left cheek twitched. Otherwise, they both managed to suppress their anger admirably.

She felt vaguely dirty about what she was about to say next, but it had to be done.

"The second problem is your wife, Agent Connelly, and her insistence on dragging the NCTC into a civil lawsuit. But I think I've come up with a solution."

"Is that so?" Richardson said neutrally. He cut his eyes toward Connelly as if to say 'let me handle this.'

"Yes. If Agent Connelly can persuade her to drop the complaint against the contractor and, of course, end her crusade against the NCTC, these letters will end up in my shredder and not in your personnel files."

She thought she saw a ghost of a smile flit across Richardson's face.

Connelly actually laughed. "You obviously don't know my wife. The idea that I might hold sway over Sasha's professional decision-making process is so wrong it's hilarious. In fact, if I told her to drop her complaint, it would virtually guarantee she pursued it."

"Still, you can try to convince her."

"He's not kidding. Sasha McCandless-Connelly is five feet of fury fueled by dogged stubbornness, Ingrid. If Leo tried to get her to drop that case the only thing that would happen is he'd be sleeping on the couch."

Leo nodded. "That's true. But I want to be very clear. Even if I *could* talk her into dismissing her complaint and giving up the idea of going after the NCTC, I wouldn't. I'm not going to interfere with her work to advance agency goals. Not now, not ever." He gave her a cool, level look. "And if you ever ask me again, you won't have the chance to censure me, because I'll be gone."

She stared back at him. "You might want to reconsider that position."

He turned away from her and bobbed his head at Richardson. "I'm sorry to taint your record with this crap, Hank."

Richardson dismissed the apology with a short head shake. "Leo, do I look like I give a rat's behind about a censure letter? I'll just add it to my collection."

"Joke all you want, but I'm obviously not cut out for this position." He removed his department-issued weapon from his shoulder holster, popped out the magazine, and placed both on Ingrid's desk. Then he tossed his old U.S. Marshal identification on the surface as well.

He turned on his heel and strode out of the office.

She waited a beat then picked up his weapon and credentials and handed them to Richardson. "I had to make the offer. The director insisted."

"But you knew he'd never go for it, right?"

"I wasn't sure, to be honest. But if he had, I'd have transferred him to another position. I don't have room for disloyalty on my team. Go find him, tell him what a cold, miserable bitch I am, and convince him to stay. You know you need him."

Richardson grinned at her. "I wouldn't say cold. More like fiery. You and Sasha are two of a kind."

She laughed. "Bite your tongue. For such a tiny person, she's turned into the largest interagency pain in the ass that I've had to deal with in a long time. You better hurry if you want to catch him before he leaves the building."

She waved her hand to shoo him out of her office. He walked out laughing under his breath.

She waited until the door closed behind him then fed the contents of the folder into her shredder.

Leo was in the lobby when he heard footsteps approaching from behind. He turned to see Hank hurrying toward him.

"Save your breath, Hank. It's not negotiable. I'm not going to tell Sasha how to practice law."

"Hold your fire. I'm not here to talk you into anything."

"Oh. Okay, good."

Hank handed him his gun and identification card. "Here. Put these away."

He stared at his boss for several seconds. "Did you not hear anything I said?"

"Seriously, holster that thing. You're in the middle of an office building."

Leo shoved the weapon in his holster and slipped the ID into his wallet. "I don't understand."

"Contrary to what Sasha may think, nobody—not the director, not Ingrid, and certainly not me—thinks that national security goals are best accomplished by automatons who follow orders to the letter. We're facing mind-blowingly evil enemies, who've proved to be endlessly creative in their schemes. We can't fight that with yes men. We need agents with the courage to take risks worth taking, the willingness to admit when policy or protocol is wrong, and the integrity to do the right thing when faced with a departmental blind spot. You've got that, in spades. You've also got one helluva feisty wife, but that's not my problem, thank the good Lord."

Leo cracked a grin. He extended his hand. Hank shook it.

"Thanks, man."

Hank waved the thanks away.

"No, I mean it. I'm honored to work with you. But I have to run. There's something I need to take care of."

"Where are you going?"

"To find my feisty wife and convince her to forgive me."

41

He found her on the playground.

She was standing behind the swing set, positioned between two swings. The twins swung back and forth in an alternating rhythm. As Finn flew up, Fiona came back. She pushed Fiona's swing with her left hand, and Finn's with her right.

He stood and watched from under a shady elm tree for a moment. The kids were laughing, open-mouthed, their heads thrown back. Sasha smiled at their shrieks of joy, but even from this distance, he saw tight worry lines creasing her forehead. Lines he'd put there.

He blew out his breath in a long, slow *whoosh* and headed across the rubberized surface.

He grasped the seat of Finn's swing and held it above

his head until Finn squealed and shouted, then he released the swing and ducked underneath it. He circled around and repeated the process with Fiona, who was already chortling in anticipation. Then he came to stand beside his wife.

"Hi."

Sasha cut her green eyes toward him. "Hi. You realize you're going to be playing Underdog with them for the next eleventy-two hours, right?"

He managed a grin. "I couldn't think of any way I'd rather spend eleventy-two hours."

She smiled and returned her gaze to the swings.

"I'm sorry I kept you in the dark. I didn't have a choice."

She arched an eyebrow and twisted her lips into a skeptical bow but said nothing. She didn't need to. It was written all over her face: *You always have a choice.*

He cleared his throat and tried again. "That's not true. I did have a choice, and I intentionally chose not to tell you I'd been ordered to kill an American civilian as part of a domestic terrorism cleanup. It would've been treason to share that information."

"I know. And it would have been a violation of the rules of professional responsibility to tell you my client was considering whether to sue the NCTC. So here we are, living with the consequences of our actions." Her voice was flat.

"I told Ingrid and Hank I wouldn't pressure you about it. You have to represent your client's interest here. I get it."

She turned and searched his face. "Do you? Even if it means Hank and Ingrid won't protect you for failing to carry out an order? You could lose your job."

"I don't care."

She shot him a disbelieving look.

"I don't," he insisted. "I told them they could fire me and prosecute me, but I refuse to interfere with your work."

"And?"

"And Hank returned my weapon and identification and told me they appreciate independent thinking." He shrugged. "But it wouldn't have mattered if he hadn't. I meant what I said."

She laughed softly. "It's like an O. Henry story."

"What do you mean?"

She reached out and pushed Finn's swing. He mirrored the action with Fiona's. The longer the dynamic duo was occupied by swaying back and forth in the bucket swings, the longer he and his wife would have to hash things out between them.

"I mean, DoGiveThrive has decided to settle with

Sentinel Solution Systems and Asher Morgan. A drawn-out lawsuit would be a distraction from their charitable mission. And they can do a lot of good with three quarters of a million dollars. It was just too tempting for Gella to pass up."

"I see."

She went on. "And I referred Sheila Anne Johnson to Mickey Collins' office—there are too many potential conflicts for me to represent her against the NCTC. She might have claims against Gella's company, for one thing. And it would complicate things between you and me, for another."

"Are you okay with that?"

"I trust Mickey to represent her with zeal. And I know he won't back down when the Justice Department starts throwing its weight around."

"That's doesn't answer my question."

"My client's satisfied. Sheila Anne is satisfied. It's not about me."

"What about us?" He sucked in a breath and waited for her answer.

What about us?

The words hit her like a kidney punch. She bit her lip and glanced down.

It seemed like a simple enough question. And, Sasha supposed, the question was simple. The answer? Not so much.

After a long moment, she lifted her eyes to meet Connelly's. "You're my husband. Their father." She gestured toward the twins. "That's more important than any of the rest of this."

"Are you sure about that?"

She held his gaze. "I am. Are you?"

He didn't answer her question but asked one of his own. "Did you think, even for a second, that I might have killed Essiah Wheaton?"

There was no point in lying. "Yes."

He blanched.

"But *only* for a second," she rushed to clarify. "I know you, Leo. You're not an assassin."

He shook his head, lost in a private thought. "I could have. If the dossier had been stronger—if he'd actually *been* a domestic terrorist ... I swore an oath ...."

She placed her hand on his forearm and pitched her voice low so the kids wouldn't pick up any of their conversation. "But you didn't. You searched your conscience, and you let it guide you. Whether you can live with the chance you might face this question again is for you to figure out. That's about your work, it's not about us."

He covered her hand with his. "But it *is* about us. What if, one day, I decide someone does deserve to die without the benefit of due process? Then your husband—their father—*will* be an assassin. What then?"

She couldn't answer that for him. She shook her head. "I don't know, Connelly. It's like we always tell the kids, actions have consequences. If you go down that path, I guess we'll deal with the fallout when it happens."

It was an unsatisfying response, and she knew it. This wasn't the equivalent to painting the dog blue or eating all your sibling's strawberries. But his hypothetical was a question for him, not for her.

He tipped his head back for a moment and scanned the cloudless blue sky.

When he returned his eyes to hers, they were a steely gray.

"I'm not sure I can live with that."

Her mouth curved into a small smile. "Well, there *is* another option. You could just quit. If your unscheduled field trip taught me anything, it's that you're a far better homemaker than I am."

He mirrored her smile, but it didn't reach his eyes. "I

thought we already knew that. And the idea does have a lot of appeal. But …."

"But I doubt that being a full-time stay-at-home dad would satisfy your need to protect and serve."

He shrugged. "Executing American citizens doesn't exactly satisfy that need, either."

She studied him. "So, don't do it. You've already drawn a line in the sand, and Ingrid and Hank backed down. And, don't forget, you *did* do something in the furtherance of national security. Fletcher Lee Holden and his merry band of lunatics won't be running guns or targeting politicians anymore."

"Not to nitpick, but *you* did that."

"If you want to get technical about it, *we* did it. But the point remains, just keep acting with integrity and don't bend. Worst-case scenario, they fire you. And then I get the house-husband of my dreams. It's a no-lose proposition."

This time his grin was genuine. "When did you get so smart?"

"*Get* so smart? I've *always been* this smart, Connelly." She laughed.

He caught her around the waist and covered her lips with his. His mouth searched hers, and even as her body responded, her mind kept working.

She knew this conversation wasn't really over. He

wouldn't be able to brush aside his doubts for good. But that was okay; they'd work through it.

In their seven years together, they'd amassed a horrific collection of baggage, ranging from murdered colleagues, murderous relatives, and deranged enemies bent on vengeance. And they'd yet to collapse under the weight of their challenges. She had no intention of allowing a job—his *or* hers—to topple them.

THANK YOU!

Sasha and Leo will back in their next adventure soon. If you enjoyed, I'd love it if you'd help introduce others to the series.

Share it. Please lend your copy to a friend.

Review it. Consider posting a short review to help other readers decide whether they might enjoy it.

Connect with me. Stop by my Facebook page at www.facebook.com/authormelissafmiller.com for book updates, cover reveals, pithy quotes about coffee, and general time-wasting.

Sign up. To be the first to know when I have a new release, sign up for my email newsletter at www.melissafmiller.com. Prefer text alerts? Text BOOKS to 636-303-1088 to receive new release alerts and updates.

While I'm busy writing the next Sasha book, if you

haven't read my Bodhi King, Aroostine Higgins or my We Sisters Three series, you can pick up the first in those series now:

ROSEMARY'S GRAVY
A WE SISTERS THREE MYSTERY
MELISSA F. MILLER
USA TODAY BESTSELLING AUTHOR

ABOUT THE AUTHOR

USA Today bestselling author Melissa F. Miller was born in Pittsburgh, Pennsylvania. Although life and love led her to Philadelphia, Baltimore, Washington, D.C., and, ultimately, South Central Pennsylvania, she secretly still considers Pittsburgh home.

In college, she majored in English literature with concentrations in creative writing poetry and medieval literature and was stunned, upon graduation, to learn that there's not exactly a job market for such a degree. After working as an editor for several years, she returned to school to earn a law degree. She was that annoying girl who loved class and always raised her hand. She practiced law for fifteen years, including a stint as a clerk for a federal judge, nearly a decade as an attorney at major international law firms, and several years running a two-person law firm with her lawyer husband.

Now, powered by coffee, she writes legal thrillers and homeschools her three children. When she's not writing, and sometimes when she is, Melissa travels around the country in an RV with her husband, her kids, and her cat.

Connect with me:

www.melissafmiller.com